THE LAST
FROM GAUL

Written by

Anton Perrick

STARbooks Press, Herndon, VA

ISBN 10: 1-934187-80-1

ISBN 13: 978-1-934187-80-7

Published in the United States by

STARbooks Press, PO Box, 711612 Herndon VA 20171.

Printed in the United States

Herndon, VA

CHAPTER 1

Simonides, a Syrian born slave trader was disappointed with his agent's report from Rome. He thought that the twenty slaves he had sent from Gaul would have sold better. But there was a common saying in Rome: "Never buy a slave from Gaul. They'll give you an argument about everything and drink all the wine in your house." He was particularly disappointed in the price he had gained for the youth he had renamed Marcius. The youth had told him his real name was Orin, but he had forgotten it. Orin came from a village in the North; one of those who had joined the revolt against Rome. Not many warriors had survived, but some young captives had been sold to Simonides.

Simonides knew exactly why Orin had been spared. Orin was almost twenty years of age when he was captured, but as he was shorter than average, slightly built, and innocent looking; he appeared younger. And Orin was, in Simonides's experienced judgment, a truly beautiful young man. The Romans, generally speaking, did not consider the Gauls a handsome race; they were too big, too pale and too difficult for their taste. But in Simonides's opinion, they produced their fair share of beauties like all other peoples. Simonides would have to admit that he was biased by his own preferences. As he was very dark skinned himself, he admired the fair skinned blonds and red heads from the North. And, Orin was one of the most handsome youths he had ever bought.

Simonides would never know that Orin was the youngest son of a queen. The last of a large family, he had been born early and smaller than average. His parents' love and a wise woman's common sense had managed to keep him alive in his first two difficult years. Then he started to grow, but his parents realized that he would never be a warrior like his older brothers and sisters. His mother, Queen Neala, a tall, beautiful warrior queen who had taken as her husband a tall, handsome chieftain, loved her youngest most of all her sons. And, he was not resented (well, not much) by his older brothers and sisters. But, he had not been trained to fight. He was too fragile, and too often ill, his mother argued. So, his mother had seen that Orin was educated by a Roman freedman. His father worried about his future, but his wife said to him "He's clever! He can be a scribe and a translator and advise his big brother when he is king," she said.

As Roman soldiers approached Orin's village, his mother had ordered the elderly and children to flee to the next village to the north. These neighbors, like all neighbors, would quarrel at times, but they would not refuse refuge to each other's elderly and young in such dangerous times. But, Orin had left it too late to flee. He had started out with the others, but turned back deciding that he was old enough to fight with his brothers and sisters.

By the time Orin reached the forest near his village, the battle was over. As Roman soldiers looted his village, he watched from behind some bushes. Orin knew there was nothing he could do except wait until the Romans started to return to their camp. Orin intended to creep through the woods and head north once the soldiers were gone. But, Orin was unlucky. Two young soldiers saw Orin move behind the bushes and started walking toward him. Orin turned and ran. Orin, if not a warrior like his brothers and sisters, could run fast when he had to, and at this moment, he had to. But, the soldiers chasing him were young and very fit, and when Orin slowed down, one of the soldiers caught up with him and tackled him from behind. Orin was knocked to the ground. Orin struggled as one of the soldiers used his superior weight and strength to pin him to the ground. Gaius caught up with his friend, Lucius. Both soldiers took a minute to get their breaths back from running.

"Let her up a bit, Lucius," Gaius said. Let's have a look at her."

During this chase, Lucius and Gaius had seen Orin only from behind, and due to his long blond braided hair, long tunic, and slight build they had assumed that that they were pursuing a young woman.

"Gaius. Why did you say the girls here aren't pretty? This one's a beauty," Lucius said.

"Only one problem, Lucius. It's a boy."

"Are you sure? It looks like a girl to me. Look at this long hair, this sweet face," Lucius said.

Orin knew Latin and understood the mocking conversation going on. He continued to struggle.

"Let go of me, you Roman pigs," he said in Latin.

The soldiers exchanged a glance.

"He understands Latin. That will make things easier."

Lucius looked at Gaius and winked.

"I won't tell anyone if you don't," Lucius said.

Lucius pushed Orin back, turned him onto his stomach, and held him down. Orin knew exactly what the soldiers were going to do to him, and although he could not move his upper body, he could move his legs, so he squirmed, wriggled and kicked. Gauis knelt down quickly and grabbed Orin's legs. He pulled Orin's legs apart.

"Pretty boy doesn't fancy us, Lucius," he sneered.

Gaius pulled up Orin's cape, then his long tunic, and pulled down his warm trousers.

"That's a pity," Lucius said. "He's the prettiest barbarian I've ever seen."

"And he smells nice and clean, too," Gaius said as he positioned himself in front of Orin's spread buttocks.

"No! Stop it! Don't! Let me go!" Orin screamed as he tried to get away from the soldiers.

Gaius quickly became erect as Orin struggled. Gaius was, after all, young, fit, and it had been a while since he and Lucius had caught such a handsome, young prisoner. That they had caught a youth rather than a woman did not really worry either of them. Gaius pushed his penis into Orin with one hard, single thrust and started to move quickly and vigorously inside him. Orin felt as if a stick had been pushing inside him, and he screamed. Gaius reached a climax quickly, and then withdrew from Orin's body. He released his hold on Orin, so he and Lucius could change positions. Then Lucius started to take his turn with Orin. He grabbed hold of Orin's legs as firmly as Gaius had done.

"No! Please! Don't! Please!" Orin whimpered.

"Pretty boy's learning some manners already," Gaius said.

Orin kept crying out as Lucius thrust inside him until he was satisfied. Thus, Orin's first sexual experience with a Roman was brutal, painful and messy. All that could be said for it was that it was over quickly. Orin did not yet know that Roman soldiers learn to rape captives quickly in case they get a barbarian's spear in the back (or, even, in a more intimate place). When they finished and had adjusted their uniforms, Orin lay shocked and hurt on the ground. As he was the youngest of his large protective family and his mother's favorite, he had never been treated roughly by anyone before.

"What now?" Lucius asked.

Gaius sighed.

"We kill him," he said.

Gaius retrieved his sword, which he had briefly put aside. As Orin saw the sword raised above his head, he instinctively raised his arm in front of his face. A golden bracelet on his wrist glistened in the sunshine.

"Wait," said Lucius.

"What is it now?" Gaius asked.

"That's gold, isn't it? He's somebody."

"No he isn't," Gaius said. "Just a minute."

Their captive wore numerous rings, many bracelets and a torque. There were all large, gold and valuable. Gaius quickly stripped the youth of his jewelry and looked at it.

"Somebody's daddy is very rich," Gauis said.

"Do they have rich people here?" Lucius asked.

"I think they have nobles and kings and stuff," Gaius said.

"Oh shit," said Lucius. "We better hand him over to some officers. They'll know what to do with him."

# # # # #

Two Roman officers looked around the deserted village.

"I thought that we'd capture a few slaves here. This was a reasonably good sized village," the senior officer Titus Gallus Naso remarked.

"It looks like as if they fled before we got here; quite clever for barbarians," his junior officer said.

"Never underestimate your enemy," Gallus Naso commented somewhat automatically.

Lucius and Gaius held Orin tightly by the arms and brought him before the officers.

"We found this one in the woods, sir. We thought he might know something," Gauis said.

The officer nodded at Gaius, and Orin was pushed into a kneeling position in front of Gallus Nason. Orin looked up at the senior officer.

"Where is everyone?" Gallus Naso asked.

"The old people and the children fled two days ago. Anyone who could not fight was ordered to go north," Orin said.

"And you're here because?" Gallus Naso asked.

In his opinion the slightly built barbarian youth looked too young to fight.

"I came back to fight with my brothers. I'm old enough," he said defiantly.

The soldiers laughed at him, but Gallus Naso felt some pity as he had a son about the youth's age back home in Rome.

"Of course you did. You're a brave lad," Gallus Naso said.

"So what do we do with him, sir?" the junior officer asked.

"He's obviously someone. Look at his clothes. And he speaks Latin well. Not many of them do. He's no peasant. He's from a noble family. When the carts arrive for the loot, put him in a cart and make sure you tie him properly."

Before dusk, the Romans marched back to their camp to eat, drink and sleep. Marcius was tied in a wagon before it set out for the Roman camp. Lucius and Gaius were told to keep an eye on the boy by Gallus Naso. Gallus Naso knew perfectly well what had happened in the woods. Orin's disheveled appearance, pale face and shocked expression showed that he had been hurt. So he said to Lucius and Gauis: "Touch him again, and I'll have you flogged."

Orin had not fought or struggled when the wagon driver had tied his wrists together and then lifted him bodily and placed him in the wagon. The wagon driver was used to captives who tried to kick, hit, scratch and bite him when he restrained them, but Orin was too exhausted and dispirited to offer any resistance. So the wagon driver did not tie him too tightly, and did not interfere when Orin reached for some covers in the cart to put over him. They traveled slowly to the Romans' camp.

When they arrived, the driver checked that Orin was still securely tied and said, "Now, stay quiet. If you behave yourself I'll bring you back some bread and water."

Then the driver went off in search of his own dinner.

Left alone, Orin started to cry as he grieved for his family, village and the only way of life he had ever known.

I'm not frightened of dying, he thought. But, I'm frightened of them torturing me to death.

Gauis came over to the wagon and looked at Orin.

"Stop that, brat. Or I'll ..." he said

"No you won't," Orin said as he looked up at Gaius. "If you hurt me again, I'll tell the officers about my jewelry. They won't let you keep it."

Gaius smiled.

"All right, pretty boy. We have a bargain. You keep your mouth shut about everything that happened earlier, and Lucius and I will see that you're looked after."

In his tent, Gallus Naso briefly consulted with his subordinate officers before dismissing them. The Parisii had left their village with such haste that they had left behind most of their crops and livestock, so the Roman troops would eat well for a while. The legate had personally searched the village's largest hut, which he correctly assumed had belonged to the village's chieftain. He was pleased to find quite a few small, exquisitely carved wooden chests containing silver and gold coins, as well as jewelry.

A rich barbarian lived here, Gallus Naso concluded, and his woman had quite good taste when it came to jewelry and clothes.

"It's a shame we didn't capture more of them," a junior officer joked to his commander privately after a meeting. "I would enjoy taming a pretty young barbarian tonight."

So would I, Gallus Naso thought.

After his meeting with his officers, Gallus Naso sent one of his soldiers to collect his dinner. Then he remembered Orin. Even though he had only questioned Orin briefly, he had noticed what a good looking youth he was. He did not really blame his soldiers for enjoying the pretty boy in the woods, except that they were supposed to be on duty. So the legate sent another soldier to bring Orin to him.

"The legate wants to talk to the prisoner," the soldier said to the wagon driver.

The wagon driver grinned.

"I bet he does more than talk to him. Selfish sod," he said.

"Rank has its privileges," the soldier commented.

The soldier found Orin under some furs and rugs in the wagon, and dragged him out. These rugs and furs had belonged to his parents, so Orin felt he was more entitled to use them than the Romans. The wagon driver had not objected, although he did tell Orin not to get any dirt on the furs.

As it was getting darker and colder, the soldier even waited for Orin to quickly wrap a large fur cape around his shoulders.

When Orin arrived at the legate's tent, Gallus Naso was sitting down to enjoy his evening meal. To one side on the table in front of him were scrolls, which Orin assumed to contain his orders and maps. In front of the commander was a large wooden bowl containing pork stew and a loaf of bread. There was a large jug of wine and water and a single cup beside the bowl. Orin was thirsty although he was too shaken by the day's events to feel particularly hungry.

Gallus Naso had removed his armor and placed a warm woolen robe over his tunic. He wondered how the local people ever got used to the climate. Then he looked at Orin wrapped in his large sable cape. As this cape had belonged to his mother, it was rather big on Orin, but it was a beautiful fur. Gallus Naso took his time looking at Orin. Orin's father had been auburn haired, but his mother's most admired physical feature had been her long, thick reddish blond hair. Orin had inherited his looks from his mother, but his hair was truly blond. Orin's hair was, in fact, the color of a field of wheat. Gallus Naso looked at Orin's fair complexion, his delicate features, and large blue eyes. Gallus Naso had seen many fair, blue eyed barbarians in his career, but he did not think he had ever seen blue eyes quite as blue as Orin's.

"Come here, boy," he said. "You must be hungry by now. Come sit on my lap, and I'll let you share my dinner."

"Sir?" Orin asked. "Do I have to?"

"Yes you do," the Roman said coldly. "I don't wish to be cruel to you since you've been obedient so far, but I can do anything I like to you. I can have you whipped to death or crucified. I can give you to my soldiers, and most of them will enjoy raping a boy like you as much as a pretty girl. Or I could ruin that lovely face of yours with a branding iron. Now, don't be foolish and come here."

Reluctantly, Orin went over to the officer and seated himself on his lap. The Roman put an arm around Orin's slim waist to steady him. He gave him his spoon and told him to eat.

Orin slowly ate some of the stew and some bread. Then he put the spoon on the table.

"Is that all you want?" Gallus Naso asked. "No wonder you're thin."

"I'm not really hungry, sir," Orin said.

Gallus Naso poured wine into his cup and handed it to Orin.

"But like all your race, you like wine," he said.

Gallus Naso let Orin have a few cups of wine, while he reached up to undo his braids and fondle his long blond hair. Then he reached under Orin's tunic and started to fondle him. Orin squirmed.

"Sir," he said.

"Have you forgotten what I said before?" the Roman asked.

"No sir," Orin said miserably.

Gallus Naso told Orin to go over to his bunk and undress. As he finished his stew and wine, he watched the young man strip. When Orin had been sitting on his lap, Gallus Naso had noticed that Orin did not seem to weigh very much, and he wondered if the youth was undernourished. But when Orin undressed it was obvious that he was not skinny, simply that he was naturally slim and delicate looking.

"You're a beautiful young man. Your skin is so fair. There isn't a mark or scar on you. You're lovely enough to warm a king's bed, or a general's. Maybe I should give you to Julius Caesar as a present, he likes variety, sexually speaking. And, you'd be an interesting change from some oily Eastern trollop. Get into bed."

Gallus Naso drained his cup of wine, and went over to Orin. He started to undress.

"Please sir," Orin said. "The soldiers in the woods … they held me down and made me do it. It hurt. Don't do that to me. Please!"

"All right, boy," the Roman said. "Lie back. I don't expect you to be experienced like a boy from the East, but I imagine lads your age in Gaul play with each other like lads everywhere else."

For extra warmth, Orin reached over and pulled his fur cape over the blankets that lay on the commander's bed. He pulled the fur over his chest, but left his arms uncovered. The youth's fair skin and blond hair looked even more striking contrasted with the almost black fur. Gallus Naso climbed into his bed. The bed was only meant for one person, so Orin turned onto his side to make room for the Roman. They faced each other in the bed. Then, Gallus Naso did something that really surprised Orin. He kissed him hungrily and passionately on the mouth as his hand descended under the covers to stroke Orin's nipples, then his belly and then his genitals. Orin was only nineteen, and he soon became erect. The Roman took hold of Orin's erect penis and gently manipulated it. He guided Orin right hand to his own semi erect penis so that Orin could do the same for him. Orin reciprocated.

"Good lad," Gallus Naso whispered. "So nice and gentle. I'll be gentle with you, too. Now, show me how much you know about sucking."

Orin had had some sexual experiences with older boys in his village, so he knew something about kissing, fondling and sucking. But he had never let his previous partner sodomize him as he feared that it would hurt. And no previous partner had been able to make Orin do anything he did not want to; after all, he was the youngest son of his tribe's queen.

So Orin did the sort of thing that he had done before. He gently took hold of Gallus Naso's erect penis and guided it into his mouth. He gently licked the tip at first, then the foreskin. He relaxed his mouth and jaw, opened his mouth, made sure his teeth were covered and started to move his mouth back and forth around Gallus Naso's erect penis. Orin knew that he was pleasing the man as the Roman moaned with pleasure now and again. Orin wondered if the officer would climax in his mouth, which he was not particularly looking forward to, but he considered it preferable to Gallus Naso using his bottom.

Instead, the Roman said, "That's enough, now lie back."

Orin did so. Gallus Naso positioned himself on top of Orin, so he could rub his penis between Orin's thighs. The Roman's belly rubbing against Orin brought Orin to climax first, but Gallus Naso climaxed soon after. Orin's skin felt sticky, but Gallus Naso had not hurt him the way the soldiers had done. Gallus Naso kissed Orin, then rolled off him.

"Good slave," he muttered.

He would have kept Orin in his bed overnight except that it was not really comfortable to have two people in his narrow bed, and he thought that Orin could try to escape. Therefore, once Orin was dressed, he called a centurion to escort him back to the wagon. Orin's feet and wrists were tied by the centurion and a rope round his neck secured him to a paling in the side of the wagon. But the centurion did not tie him too tightly, so Orin could move a little. Once the centurion had gone, he also was able to reach out and pull more furs over his body, so he was not cold overnight.

# # # # #

The fort commander, Sextus Domitius Avitus, happened to be near the main gate when the wagon trundled into the fort's yard. He went over to the wagon driver.

"No captives?" he asked as these sort of wagons usually arrived at the fort with a pathetic train of chained captives behind them.

"Just one, sir," the wagon driver said.

"One! Where is he?" Domitius Avitus asked.

"He's tied up in the back, sir."

"Why isn't he in chains?" Domitus Avitus asked.

"He's only a lad, sir. He's been no trouble. I think he's a bit slow," the wagon driver said.

"Let's have a look at him," he said.

The driver told Orin to come out of the wagon. Orin had been half asleep and once he was standing on the ground he pushed his long hair back from his face. He looked quite young as he did so. Sextus Domitius Avitus was not sexually interested in young men himself, but he knew a captive who would sell for a good price when he saw one.

"He looks like a strong wind would blow him away," he said to the wagon driver. "But he looks very tame."

Orin did not like being referred to as if he were an animal, and he glanced at the commander for a brief moment before staring at the ground again.

The fort commander laughed.

"He understands Latin. That will make him worth more. Lock him in a storeroom near the kitchen. And make sure he has food, water and blankets. He might get ill if he's penned with the other captives."

So Orin was chained in the corner of a storeroom. That afternoon, the wagon driver brought him water and some sort of porridge in a bowl. Orin looked at the porridge doubtfully. The wagon driver laughed.

"You better get used to that. That's what most slaves live on."

"Am I a slave now?" Orin asked.

"It's better to be a live slave than a dead warrior."

"Is it?" Orin asked.

"Yes. Listen to me, lad. You're young. You're smart enough to know not to be difficult. You understand and speak Latin. You're good looking. You'll be a valuable slave. Romans don't treat valuable slaves badly. Think about it."

The next morning, the commander sent a message to a Syrian born slave trader he knew. This slave trader was a good business man who had an understanding with Domitius Avitus that he had first choice of any captives arriving at the garrison. Simonides considered that he dealt in quality rather than quantity when he dealt in slaves. He preferred to buy young, healthy attractive captives who were suitable to be trained as household slaves for rich Romans. Simonides was impressed with Orin's appearance especially his huge blue eyes, long blond hair and fair skin. Orin was frightened, but tried not to show it.

Simonides had selected and purchased from Domitius Avitus seven young captives that morning, two young women and five youths, but he paid most for Orin. Simonides would not send Orin and his other slaves to Rome immediately. He sent his slaves in lots of about twenty by ship. They arrived in better health that way. From Simonides's point of view, the revolt in Gaul had not been as successful as he wished as the Gauls seemed to have the annoying idea that it was preferable to die in battle than be taken prisoner and enslaved.

Odd people, Simonides thought.

Simonides kept his slaves in a converted barn. The slaves were kept chained and guarded, but the place was kept clean and the captives supplied with adequate food, water, clothing and bedding. A healthy slave might not be happy, but a healthy slave sold better than one that looks ill and mistreated. But Simonides did not have his latest acquisition chained in the barn. He gave him to his steward with orders to have Orin fed, rubbed down with Simonides's favorite perfumed oil, and bathed. A generous meal was set before Orin who was very hungry by this time. He drank all the wine in a jug set on the table when he was told to do so. Orin did not mind the bath very much, but he objected to the rub down with oil. The steward gave him a hard warning slap across the face. A naked Orin was escorted to and locked in what was obviously Simonides's bedroom. The room was luxuriously decorated. There was also, Orin noted, a strap on a hook beside the trader's bed. Orin examined it. It did not look that threatening; the sort of thing used on domestic servants, but in an experienced hand, he imagined it would sting well enough. It started to grow dark and colder, so Orin slid into Simonides's bed. He was too tired to stay out of it.

Simonides unlocked the door and came into his bedroom. He was wearing a red, elaborate embroidered robe. It was the sort of thing that Orin had never seen before, but Orin had never been to Syria. In any other circumstances, he might have laughed. Simonides came over to the bed as Orin sat up. He sat on his bed and stroked Orin's arm. Simonides was a large, fleshy man but powerful looking. Orin knew that he had no real chance of fighting him off. Simonides toyed with the youth's long blond hair.

"What's your name, little Gaul?" Simonides asked.

"Orin, sir," Orin said politely.

"Orin, master," Simonides corrected.

"Yes, master," said Orin.

"What does it mean?" Simonides asked.

"White haired. When I was born, my mother said that my hair was white, although it's darker now," Orin explained.

"Not much darker. I thought you must be from a German tribe when Domitius Avitus first showed you to me. But you speak some Latin, so you're obviously a Gaul. A Roman owner will appreciate the fact that you will be able to understand his orders. But, you'll need a name more appealing to Romans when I sell you. I want the buyers to know they're not buying an uneducated savage. I think I'll call you Marcus, no maybe not, every second Roman you meet is called Marcus. I'll call you Marcius. Some slaves are called Marcius."

Orin nodded.

Orin was beginning to understand that if he wanted to survive he could no longer think of himself as a prince of the Parisii, the descendant of generations of chieftains, but a barbarian slave named Marcius. Orin knew that he had no choice any more. Simonides pulled his robe off over his head. He wore no loincloth underneath, and he was already aroused. He got into bed beside Marcius, and for a while, he cuddled and fondled the frightened youth. He was in no hurry to enjoy him.

"Do you know what I want, Marcius?" the slave trader asked.

I would have to very stupid not to know what this big, randy bastard wants, Marcius thought. I've been ordered to strip, bathe and been locked naked in his bedroom. I don't imagine he wants to discuss the weather with me.

But Marcius knew not to give any indication as to what he was thinking. He did not know if a Syrian born slave trader could torture and kill him with impunity as the Roman commander, Gallus Naso, could have done if he disobeyed him, but he was not prepared to take the risk. Marcius remembered what the wagon driver had said to him about valuable slaves.

This man makes his living from dealing in slaves, Marcius thought. If he wants to sell me for a good price, it is in his interest not to mistreat me. It's just sex. If I'm quiet and do what he tells me, he might not be cruel to me.

"Master," Marcius said. "You don't have to hurt me. I'll do what you tell me ... It's just ... I don't know what you like."

Simonides smiled. He considered that a beautiful young man like Marcius could not possibly be a virgin. Marcius had been captured by Roman soldiers, after all, and if someone had not raped him by now, the Roman army had changed since Simonides was captured and enslaved when young. But Marcius was obviously nervous, and Simonides had no wish to hurt him unnecessarily. Marcius was not being defiant or disobedient, he was simply saying honestly that he was frightened.

And in his situation, what captive would not be afraid? Simonides asked himself. At least he has enough common sense to know it's pointless to give me a fight about it. And his shyness along with his blond good looks make him very appealing, Simonides thought.

"That's fine, little Gaul. Don't be nervous. I don't expect you to be an expert. I'll show you what to do," Simonides said.

Despite Marcius's fear, Simonides's experienced fingertips caressing Marcius's body had an inevitable result. Then the Syrian moved down the bed to take the youth in his mouth. Marcius was soon aroused and moaning. Simonides turned Marcius over onto his stomach, and said, "Spread your legs, little Gaul."

"Master," Marcius said uneasily.

"I understand, Marcius. Some soldiers hurt and frightened you, but I'm going to take my time and be careful and gentle with you," Simonides said.

Simonides massaged Marcius's back and bottom for a while to relax him. Simonides was a sensuous person and he enjoyed touching his new slave's beautiful body. Simonides felt Marcius's muscles relax under his touch. Then he reached for a jar of ointment that he kept under his bed and carefully applied some ointment to Marcius's bottom. Marcius winced as a finger carefully entered him to apply more of the lubricant internally, but he did not cry out or resist. Simonides was not just preparing Marcius for sex, he was also checking that he had not been injured by soldiers and was trying to estimate just how experienced Marcius was.

As he withdrew his finger he said to Marcius, "I see, Marcius. No wonder the soldiers hurt you. Are you still sore?"

"No, master," Marcius said.

Marcius had been confined at the Roman garrison for almost a week, and he had been left alone by the soldiers there. He had been sore after being raped, but he felt better now. Simonides patted Marcius's bottom pleased that Marcius had not attempted to deceive him.

"I see you washed yourself thoroughly in the bath. That's important. A slave like you has to be fussy about cleanliness."

Simonides then lavishly applied some ointment to himself. He leaned over and kissed Marcius's shoulder.

"I'm sorry if it hurts, but you'll get used to it," Simonides said.

He entered Marcius who could not help crying out. At least it did not hurt as much as when the two soldiers had raped him. Once Simonides was completely inside Marcius, he paused, so Marcius could adjust and relax his muscles. Simonides began to slowly thrust inside Marcius, who moaned occasionally, but did not struggle. Simonides thrust inside Marcius until he climaxed, rested, then withdrew from Marcius's body and rolled onto the other side of the bed. He reached out to Marcius, turned him onto his back, and moved beside him. Lying on his side, and supporting himself on one elbow, he reached out and pushed Marcius's hair out of his face and looked at him.

"Now, that wasn't too bad, was it, Marcius?" he asked.

"No master," Marcius said.

"Did it hurt?" Simonides asked.

"Yes, but not like before," Marcius said.

"It will get easier for you every time," Simonides said.

He fell asleep almost immediately, and Marcius fell asleep soon after him.

In the morning, Simonides guided the sleepy youth's hand to him, while he dealt with Marcius's own erection. Marcius did his best to please Simonides relieved that he was not asking anything more from him. But after bathing and then breakfast together, Simonides ordered Marcius chained in the barn with his other slaves. Simonides's steward escorted Marcius and gave him a pair of brown sandals, a loincloth, a dull brown tunic and a coarse looking woolen gray cloak. These humble garments were at least clean, in fact, they had the faded look of clothes that had been washed many times and worn by many previous owners.

"What about my clothes?" Marcius asked.

"Your clothes are too heavy for this climate, and too good for a slave to wear," the steward said.

Simonides had instructed his steward that Marcius should be treated like any other slave, so he learned his place. In Simonides's view, Marcius should one day sell for a tidy sum, but he needed to be humble and obedient to do so. From his reactions, Simonides had surmised that Marcius was not quite as young and innocent as he appeared to be, but he was obviously not very sexually experienced. Simonides could imagine an over protective mother in Marcius's past.

Marcius's mother is one of those formidable warrior women they breed here, Simonides thought.

Two days later, an evening with Marcius did not go to Simonides's satisfaction. Simonides had sent for him in the evening after dining. He had had a long, busy day, and he wanted quick sex and some sleep. He beckoned to Marcius. Simonides put his hands on Marcius's shoulders to push him onto his knees. He sat on the edge of his bed and grabbed Marcius's upper arm to pull his face toward him. Then Simonides lifted his own tunic with his free hand. It was so abrupt and crude that Marcius felt nauseous and disgusted.

He pulled back from Simonides and said, "No. I won't do it."

Simonides frowned. He hauled Marcius up with one hand, pushed him over onto the bed and reached for his strap with the other.

Marcius squirmed and cried as Simonides administered ten or so hard whacks to Marcius's buttocks. In Simonides's opinion it would be a shame to permanently mark such lovely, fair skin, but he knew that he would leave some red stripes on Marcius's bottom. He let the youth up from the bed. Marcius's hands went to rub his stinging bottom.

"Get back on your knees in front of me, slave," Simonides ordered.

From his kneeling position, Marcius looked up at Simonides's face and saw that he still looked angry, and more importantly, he still had the strap in his right hand.

"Please, master. I'm sorry. You startled me. I did not know what to do," Marcius whispered as he knelt in front of his owner. Simonides calmed down, let go of his strap, and reached his hand down to under Marcius chin.

"Now, Marcius," Simonides said in a kinder tone of voice. "I make allowances because you're young, and you have not been a slave very long. But you must not defy me. You have to try your best to please me. Otherwise, you're no use to me."

Marcius was shocked as well as hurt as he had never been beaten by anyone before.

"I'm sorry, master. I won't do it again," Marcius muttered.

Simonides patted Marcius's shoulder and said, "Now try to do what I did to you last night."

Marcius moved closer to the Syrian. Gently he lifted the front of his Simonides's tunic, and pulled down slightly his loincloth to free Simonides's erect penis. Marcius gently guided the penis into his mouth while he closed his eyes. Gently he licked and manipulated Simonides's foreskin in a way he hoped he would like then started to move his mouth back and forth around Simonides's erect penis. Marcius got into a rhythm, and Simonides was pleased with him.

"That's better. Good. Good slave. You're being my good pretty boy," he murmured as he stroked Marcius's hair.

Marcius was trying to please Simonides. He knew that he would use the strap on him again if he did not please him. Marcius took semen from Simonides into his mouth, but he managed to swallow only a little before he could turn his head to the side and spit most of it onto the floor. He wiped his mouth with the back of his hand.

He looked anxiously at Simonides, unsure if that was what he wanted him to do.

Simonides smiled. He took Marcius into his arms and into bed. Then he said, "Now, that wasn't so terrible, was it?"

"No, master," Marcius said.

"It didn't hurt, did it, Marcius?" he asked

"No master," Marcius said.

"Did it taste horrible?" Simonides asked.

"No, master," Marcius said.

"So I haven't harmed you, have I?" Simonides asked.

The Syrian went to sleep.

While he belonged to Simonides, during the day, Marcius was chained in the stables with about twenty or so other slaves. From their clothing, coloring and their whispered remarks to each other, he worked out that they were nearly all young Gauls from various tribes. The captives were grouped according to age and gender. In one corner, a small group of girls and young women huddled together. There were more boys and young men chained together. None of these young captives were older than Marcius, in fact, some were children. There was a much smaller group of men aged in their thirties and forties who from their simple tunics and broad shoulders appeared to be workmen. They were in fact craftsmen who Simonides considered would sell for a good price in Rome. The Romans sneered at the Gauls and considered them barbarians, but as soon as they started trading with them, they discovered that among the Gauls there were many skilled silversmiths and goldsmiths.

Marcius was handed over by Simonides's steward to a huge Phoenician who was in charge of the slaves in the barn.

"Keep this one separate from the others," the steward said.

"Why? Is he ill?" the guard asked.

"The boss's latest bum boy," the steward said with a shrug.

Marcius was treated the same as the other slaves in the barn by the guards, no better, but no worse. Like the others, he was escorted to the latrine and slaves' bath house at regular intervals. Twice a day he, like the other slaves, was given a loaf of dark bread and a large beaker of water. Simonides did not starve his slaves, although the food they received was very basic. Marcius noticed how quiet and subdued all the young people in barn were. He understood why the first time one of the older men sneered at one of the guards when told to do something and the man received a few hard lashes across his back. The man accepted his punishment with a certain grim resignation, but Marcius saw how frightened the younger slaves were when the man was whipped. The guards all carried on their belts vicious looking, multi-thonged whips of a kind that could easily cut a person's flesh. The strap that Simonides kept on a hook beside his bed looked like a toy compared to these sorts of whips, but Marcius instinctively knew that if he disobeyed or displeased Simonides he was quite capable of using a whip on him.

The atmosphere of weary despair among the captives was to do with more than just the fear of the guards and their whips.

This is what a defeated and dying race look like, Marcius thought, and he was glad that his mother had not survived to see her people reduced to this.

Simonides kept Marcius for a few months. At the end of his working day, he had Marcius sent to his private bathroom. Marcius was always stunned at the comfort and beauty of Simonides's bathroom. Marcius always tried to keep his body clean, but his experience of bathing, like the rest of his tribe, was to soap and rinse his body quickly in a cold mountain stream in summer and wash in a bathtub of heated water in winter. It took some time for Marcius to become accustomed to warm, scented bath water in a heated room. He would have enjoyed the experience except that Simonides always bathed with him, and

Simonides liked to treat Marcius as if he were some sort of bath toy.

The first time they bathed together Simonides soaped up his hands with some sort of lotion from a small ceramic bottle and started to wash Marcius's chest and belly. Marcius accepted this, but he really yelped when Simonides hand slid down to his genitals.

"Master," Marcius said. "I'm not a child. I can wash myself there."

Simonides grinned.

"I like touching you there as you so modestly express it. I can do anything I like to you, little Gaul. Because I let you share my bed, don't think you're any different to any of my other slaves," Simonides said.

"I don't, master. I don't expect to be treated differently," Marcius said quickly.

"Romans love to bathe, and any master who buys you will probably take you to his bath as well as his bed. That is another thing you will have to get used to," Simonides said.

Simonides passed Marcius a large sea sponge.

"Now wash me like I have you. I like it when you touch me with your soft, small hands. I'm not a modest little darling like you," Simonides said.

So Marcius put the soapy lotion on his hands and washed his master's large body. Simonides was very hairy, and he made Marcius soap and rinse his back at least twice. Marcius's touch aroused him as usual, and Simonides was soon fully erect.

"Stand up, slave" he said. "And bend over the side of the bath."

Marcius did so, but he could not help being frightened. Although the warm water had relaxed him, and he was more accustomed to being used sexually by his owner, this time Simonides did not use any lubricating oil when entering Marcius. Marcius's discomfort was added to by the fact that in this position Simonides's weight pushed Marcius's chest and the side of his face against the hard mosaic floor. To his relief, Simonides used him and reached his climax quickly. Marcius was not sure if Simonides was treating him like this to punish him, or had been too aroused to care if he hurt his slave or not.

Bathing with his master became part of Marcius's daily routine, which he never grew to like, but he did not dare complain about it. Simonides also liked to dine with Marcius in his private dining room. When he had guests, Simonides dined lying on a couch in the Roman fashion, but, privately, he preferred to sit or lie on cushions in front of a low table with Marcius by his side.

Simonides also took the opportunity to teach Marcius the names of the various dishes he shared with him. For Simonides intended to sell Marcius to a Roman aristocrat who would appreciate a graceful, pretty, obedient blond youth as a cup bearer serving at his table. He also taught Marcius to mix wine, warm water and spices in a jug before pouring the wine in his master's cup. As Marcius was a Gaul, and Gauls drank their wine without added water, Marcius thought this a silly thing to do to good quality wine, but he knew better than to make a critical comment on Greek and Roman customs. But most of Marcius's family would have said: "Wine is a fine drink, so is water. But why would anyone mix the two?"

One evening when Marcius had dined with Simonides and Simonides seemed in a particularly mellow mood, he said, "Master, may I ask you a question?"

"If it's not impertinent, little Gaul," Simonides said.

"Are you going to send me to Rome, master?" he asked.

"Of course," Simonides replied.

"Could you sell me to someone here in Massalia?" Marcius asked.

"Who?" Simonides asked.

"There are Greek merchants and Roman settlers here. Can't you sell me to one of them?" Marcius asked.

"A merchant or settler here buys strong burly laborers for heavy physical work. You are not suited to such work."

"What sort of work am I suited to, master?" Marcius asked.

"I am teaching you to be a cup bearer and page boy. At the moment, you are more decorative than useful, but you are learning quickly. Rich Romans love their dinner parties, and they love being waited on and pampered by pretty slaves like you. A Roman owner will teach you what he expects from you. If you are lucky, you're master will grow fond of you and treat you well. Some pretty boys like you do very well in Rome in the long run."

"I could be sold to a cruel master," Marcius said.

"You must pray to your gods that that does not happen, little Gaul," Simonides said.

"Could you keep me here with you, master? I'm obedient, aren't I? You're pleased with me most of the time, aren't you? I try to be a good slave. I try to please you," Marcius said.

"I know you do, Marcius. But I'm a businessman, and I will get a better price for you in Rome than here in Massalia," Simonides said.

"But," Marcius started to say.

"That's enough, slave. Don't argue with me. This discussion is finished. You don't have a say in your future. Your life will be very simple from now on as you will never need to

CHAPTER 2

Later, Marcius became part of a shipment of about twenty Gallic slaves to Rome. The Gauls where aged between twelve and forty years of age and included skilled craftsmen and attractive youths and young women intended to be trained as domestic servants. As Marcius would later realize, Simonides supplied captives for the more expensive part of the slave market. If a Roman wanted strong workers for his mines or fields, he went to another slave trader.

But Simonides's agent did not think Marcius would sell that well. He considered that buyers would see how good looking he was, but by the time Marcius arrived in Rome, he looked very thin, pale and fragile. This was solely due to sea sickness during his voyage to Rome, but prospective buyers would not know that.

After all, the agent thought, a beautiful unhealthy slave is no use to anyone. Gordius the gladiator, and his manager, Antonius, attended the auction the morning that Marcius was offered for sale. People glanced at the massive gladiator who came originally from Macedonia (or was it Thrace?). Gordius was almost seven feet tall, a superb natural fighter and had survived enough fights to become a favorite of the mob. He had earned prize money and bought his freedom. Now, he trained younger gladiators. He was built like a large tree, and some people assumed that he was about as bright as a large tree. He was immensely strong but agile, and fighting came naturally to him. His manager, Antonius, had purchased him when he was just another prisoner of war, seen his potential and trained him for the arena. After a few years, Gordius bought his freedom from Antonius, but Antonius remained his friend, and, as they had agreed, a percentage of what Gordius earned as a trainer he paid to Antonius.

Gordius had looked at the “pretty blond lad” from Gaul before the auction. He had noticed Marcius sitting chained in a group of young slaves behind the auction block. He walked over to Simonides’s agent.

“I’d like to look at that little blond one properly,” he said.

Marcius was unchained, and Simonides’s agent escorted him to a small office. The agent understood that when a prospective buyer was interested in a household slave as Gordius obviously was, he expected to examine the slave closely. The assistant ordered Marcius to strip naked in front of Gordius. When Marcius hesitated, the agent soundly slapped Marcius’s buttocks.

“Take it easy,” Gordius said. “Does he understand Latin?”

“Yes, he does,” the agent said. “He’s just being difficult.”

“I don’t think so,” said Gordius. “He’s frightened, and he’s not sure what to do.”

Simonides’s agent realized that the massive gladiator was genuinely interested in Marcius, and he knew that describing a slave as difficult was not exactly the best way of getting a good price for him.

“As you say, sir. He’s shy and he has not been a slave for long. I should not be so critical; it’s not like this one has needed much in the way of discipline, not like some of them. See for yourself, sir. Turn around, Marcius,” the agent said.

Marcius was by now naked, and he turned to show Gordius his back and buttocks. Although there were a couple of marks on Marcius, there were no permanent scars of any kind on his skin. It was obvious that Marcius had never had the sort of whipping that cut the skin and left scars, which Gordius knew was fairly unusual for a slave.

“It’s all right, lad,” Gordius said as he stepped closer to Marcius and lightly ran his right hand over Marcius’s shoulder and down his back to see how he would respond. Marcius cringed slightly, but he did not move away from Gordius. Since his arrival in Rome, he had been stripped and groped by a few potential buyers. He had learned very quickly that if he did not cooperate, Simonides's agent would cane him as soon as the buyer left the office.

"He's got a gorgeous little body," the assistant said with a grin. "But he's not that experienced. If you're looking for someone who knows all the tricks, we have some Greek boys ..."

"I'm not looking for a boy like that," Gordius said. "He's very pale. Is he ill?"

"Nothing serious or contagious, sir," the agent said quickly. "He'll never be a sailor. He had a bad trip across from Massalia, but the surgeon says he'll be fine."

Gordius had examined Marcius too closely for Marcius's comfort and peace of mind. Even Marcius, who came a family of tall people, was impressed – impressed and intimidated.

Oh no, thought Marcius.

Antonius hesitated, but Gordius insisted on buying Marcius. Since Gordius had bought his freedom, he had decided that he wanted a slave of his own. Antonius and Gordius had discussed this many times before attending the auction that morning.

"Why can't you take one of the kitchen boys?" Antonius asked Gordius wearily one day.

"Had them," Gordius muttered.

"What? All of them?" Antonius asked.

"Well. The ones I like," Gordius said.

This was true. No kitchen slave had the temerity to say no when approached by Gordius. Other gladiators were scared of Gordius, and most of the trainers.

At the arena where they worked there were numerous youths and young women who cooked, cleaned, served meals, and ran errands for the gladiators and trainers (as well as providing more intimate services).

"Couldn't I just buy you a puppy?" Antonius suggested to Gordius.

"No," said Gordius. "I want a slave of my own."

For Gordius had an ambition. One day he was going to be rich enough to buy a mansion among the snobs and keep them awake all night holding riotous parties. And he wanted to own a few pretty youths (and maybe a couple of dancing girls) for these parties. As he was about thirty and very fit, he thought he could cope with that sort of lifestyle in the future.

All right, thought Antonius, as ambitions go, it's not exactly praiseworthy, but at least Gordius aspires to something. Antonius just wanted a peaceful retirement one day. Gordius considered that he had to start somewhere to achieve his ambition. He was free, he had won prize money, and Antonius was helping him invest and save.

When Marcius went up the stairs of the auction platform, he was so nervous that he managed to trip on the top step and stumble across the platform. Some in the small crowd attending the auction laughed.

Wonderful, the auctioneer thought. I'm trying to sell him as a cup bearer and he's naturally clumsy. People love having wine and food spilled on them when they're dining.

Still, the auctioneer was a professional and did his best to create interest in Marcius. In the auctioneer's opinion, Marcius did not help matters by standing with his shoulders hunched staring down at some imaginary spot on the platform in front of his feet. Marcius did not stare at the crowd sullenly and resentfully like some barbarian slaves when auctioned, but the auctioneer did not think he had ever seen anyone look more miserable. If the auctioneer had been standing closer to Marcius and not been so busy, he would have hissed in his ear, "Stand up straight, and let the buyers see your face, or I'll thrash the living daylights out of you".

The auctioneer was therefore relieved when Gordius made the first bid. Marcius looked up briefly, and some of the buyers at the front of the crowd saw his magnificent, large bright blue eyes for the first time. One bid came from the owner of one of Rome's more notorious boy brothels. Then a well painted and over dressed middle aged widow, who since her husband's death now lived frankly for pleasure, put in her bid. Her maid, who always accompanied her mistress when shopping, whispered, "He looks a bit puny, mistress."

"I'll be gentle with him," her mistress joked.

Some in the crowd laughed. An off duty soldier near them turned to his friend and said, "If that's a Gaul, why did it take Caesar so long to conquer them?"

"He's not typical. He's a baby Gaul. They're like puppies, cute when little, but they grow up fierce."

"Nothing fierce about that one."

"Some of them know the war is over."

The auctioneer felt he was losing control of the crowd by this stage, so he was relieved when Gordius put in a final bid which he quickly accepted.

So, Gordius bought Marcius at what Gordius considered a reasonable price. Marcius was chained and manacled before being handed over to Gordius who led him through the market place. Marcius considered this somewhat excessive. As he looked at Gordius's broad back he knew he would never dare run away from him.

He could tear me into little pieces with his bare hands, Marcius thought miserably.

Gordius beamed with pleasure as he led his new slave to the arena.

Exactly as if I'd bought him a puppy, Antonius thought.

Antonius insisted that the arena's surgeon examine Marcius.

"Why?" asked Gordius.

"Gordius," Antonius said rather sternly. "You don't want to kill him, do you? That would be a terrible waste of your money."

"As long as everyone knows he's mine," Gordius said.

"Yes, he's all yours," Antonius agreed.

The surgeon spoke to Marcius and examined him gently. He realized that he was not seriously ill, but needed rest and nourishment. He spoke with Gordius. The surgeon had patched up Gordius after many fights and Gordius respected the doctor's opinion.

"Three days," the doctor suggested. "Leave him with me for three days. Then I'll send him to your cell ... er ... room."

Gordius grumbled but agreed.

So Marcius rested for three days, was fed nourishing food and wine, and was made to drink strange herbal concoctions. On the last day, the surgeon gave him a small jar of ointment. To Marcius, it looked and smelt vaguely familiar.

"You put it," the surgeon began to explain.

"I know what you do with it," Marcius interrupted.

The surgeon had to laugh.

"You're not such a virgin as all that," he commented. "Despite that innocent face. Now, look lad. Gordius is not a monster, but he's … well ... a simple soul. Don't argue with him. He owns you now, and he will expect obedience from you. Antonius and I will keep an eye on you. Between us, we have some influence on Gordius."

A rested Marcius was escorted by a trainer to Gordius's room one evening at dusk. Gordius had enjoyed a pleasant meal, a few cups of wine (not too many) and was looking forward to his first night with his little pet from Gaul. Gordius's room was simply furnished but comfortable. There was a brazier for heating, a simple table with two benches, a large chest for storing clothes, and a large bed with plenty of covers in a corner. Gordius sat on his bed waiting for Marcius. As it was a warm evening, he was wearing only his loincloth. Undressed, to Marcius, Gordius looked even more massive than before. But there was no fat anywhere on Gordius's body; his bulk was all muscle.

And scars, Marcius thought. He must have survived many battles and fights.

Gordius took Marcius by the hand and made him sit beside him on the bed. In the light provided by the lamps and candles, Gordius considered that Marcius looked even prettier than he did in the daylight. The rest and food had also done Marcius good, and he now had some color in his cheeks. He had lost that ill, drained look he had had previously, although he looked nervous. Gordius made Marcius stand up, pulled his tunic up over his head and removed his loincloth. Marcius was frightened and he whispered, "Master, please don't hurt me."

Gordius looked into Marcius's young, frightened face. Gordius was so much taller than Marcius that even though he was still sitting down his face and Marcius's face were on the same level. Although Gordius would not be considered handsome by most people, he was certainly not ugly. Marcius's mother would have described Gordius as a man with an honest face. More importantly for Marcius, now that he was so close to him, Marcius saw that Gordius did not look like he was a stupid brute, as Marcius had assumed a gladiator should look like up close.

"I did not buy you to hurt you, little Gaul," Gordius said soothingly. "I used to be a slave myself. I know what it's like to be bought and sold, and owned by someone."

Gordius sat Marcius on the bed and started to caress him. Marcius was surprised at the gentle way the big gladiator touched him, and the obvious pleasure it gave him to do it. And the youth's fair smooth skin did please Gordius. Marcius also had fine blond body hair which, if not that plentiful, proved that Marcius was physically mature. Gordius placed Marcius in his bed and then stripped off himself. Marcius realized why the surgeon had not seemed overly worried about him. For although Gordius was built on massive lines, the gods had not been overly generous in one department. If Gordius's penis was smaller than average, he did not worry about it. If anyone had ever been foolish enough to comment on this fact, he would have said, "It works fine." But this fact was of considerable relief to Marcius. Gordius spent a good deal of time caressing Marcius's beautiful young body, paying particular attention to Marcius's genitals.

"Even your prick is nice looking," Gordius said. "And that's not something you can say about many lads."

In return, Marcius caressed Gordius with his fingers and mouth in the ways the slave trader had liked.

At one stage, Gordius moved down the bed to lick and suck Marcius's penis and bring him to full erection. When Gordius was fully erect himself and ready, he turned Marcius onto his stomach, but positioned Marcius with his knees bent, his bottom raised, and his penis resting against a lump in the bedclothes. Marcius tried to remember the things that Simonides had said to him in bed. Marcius turned his face on the side on the bed, and tried to relax.

Simonides had told Marcius, "Relax and breathe. Don't struggle or protest, and try not to make too much noise. Your master will be happy with you then. You have to show you're willing and obedient."

Gordius knelt between Marcius's spread legs and positioned himself in front of his anus. He moistened two finger tips and gently moistened Marcius's hole before gently inserting a finger inside. Marcius gasped.

Gordius was surprised. Although Marcius looked young and innocent, he was not a child and certainly not a virgin.

Where has he been all his life? In a cave in Gaul by himself? Gordius wondered.

He spread Marcius's cheeks and entered him. Gordius moved slowly and carefully until he was completely inside Marcius. He then paused and stroked Marcius's hair.

"Are you all right, pretty one?"

"Yes master," Marcius managed to say.

He was hurting Marcius, but Marcius had applied some ointment before coming to Gordius, and as Gordius was smaller than Simonides, he was not hurting him as much as the slave trader had. Gordius settled into a rhythm of slow, smooth thrusts inside Marcius. These movements forced Marcius's erect penis to rub against the soft bedclothes. Marcius was aware of two sensations; the thrusts in his bottom, but also the building excitement in his penis as he moved against the bedclothes. Despite some pain, Marcius climaxed on the blankets. Gordius grinned and whispered in his ear as he continued his own thrusts, "So you like that, do you, lovely boy? I like you," he said.

Gordius quickened his movements and reached his own climax while a somewhat confused Marcius lay still waiting for him to finish. Gordius climaxed with quite a loud groan, then rested briefly.

Gordius withdrew from Marcius's body, then rolled off him and returned to one side of the bed. Gordius intended to go to sleep almost immediately. Sleepily, Gordius leaned over to give the youth a kiss and realized that there were tears on Marcius's cheeks.

"Did it hurt that much? I wasn't trying to hurt you," Gordius said.

"I know you weren't, master," said Marcius. "But I'm not used to it, and it hurts. I'm sorry, master," he said.

"What are you apologizing for?" Gordius asked. "I knew you weren't a slut when I saw you at the market."

Gordius opened his arms wide and took Marcius into them. Marcius rested his head on Gordius's chest.

"You seemed to enjoy it a bit, Marcius," Gordius said.

"I know. And I don't understand why. It scares me, and it hurts," Marcius said.

"You're young and you're inexperienced. No wonder you're confused. I promise you that I won't use your bottom until you feel more comfortable about it. There's plenty of other ways we can have fun until you feel safer with me. I'm going to care for you, Marcius. I'm going to treat you well, and protect you. Now, go to sleep and try not to worry," Gordius said.

Days later, Marcius considered that the Syrian slave trader's lessons were not wasted. Gordius's sexual desires were straight forward like the man, and Marcius wanted to please him. Gordius only penetrated Marcius's buttocks when Marcius was willing, relaxed and very well lubricated. Gordius was fine with that. Gordius even liked to kiss and cuddle Marcius. Marcius did not much care for Gordius's somewhat sloppy kisses, but it seemed unwise, and ungrateful, to resist them or complain. He realized that the huge gladiator was being kind to him when he was under no obligation to do so.

Although, at the start, there was one problem. After their first night together, Marcius asked Gordius what work he should do during the day. Gordius was new to the whole experience of being a slave owner, and he had to think about this. Gordius trained gladiators during the day, and Marcius could not just sit around in his room waiting for him. The idea of a slave sitting around was distinctly non Roman.

"You could ... um ... sweep the floor and scrub the table and benches," Gordius suggested. "And make the bed," he added. Gordius was beginning to feel quite pleased with himself.

"And look after the lamps. You can do that, can't you?" he asked.

"Yes, I can do that, master," replied Marcius.

It did not sound that difficult to Marcius, but neither of them really had the slightest idea about cleaning.

As Gordius went to work, Marcius went to the kitchens to ask for supplies to clean Gordius's room. As he spoke to the kitchen manager, he realized that he did not even know what he would need. The manager smiled and called over an older kitchen slave to help him. He sent them off with cloths, scrubbing brush, mop, bucket and a broom.

That little Gaul has never done a day's work in his life, the kitchen manager thought. But, at least, he's keen.

The work was not quite as easy as Marcius had imagined, although there was no clutter, Gordius had allowed a fair amount of dust to accumulate. He had simply not noticed. The older slave showed Marcius how to clean, fill and relight the lamps and how to build a fire in the brazier for when it would be needed. They made the bed. Marcius joined the other kitchen slaves for an early lunch, so they could help the cooks prepare a larger meal for the gladiators and trainers. The head chef noticing the new lad looking somewhat at a loss, set him simple tasks such as chopping vegetables and taking plates and jugs of watered down wine into the dining room. Gordius was pleasantly surprised to see Marcius working quietly with the other youths. After the meal, Marcius helped with clearing tables and washing dishes. Marcius was not very skilled at these tasks, but he was willing to learn. He also liked being with the other young slaves. Marcius was sent away and told to come back later to help with the evening meal.

Before the head chef started his afternoon work, he sat down for a cup of wine with the kitchen manager.

"That's a pretty new one," the chef said referring to Marcius. "Useless, but pretty. What's his name?"

"His name is Marcius, but hands off. He belongs to Gordius. He bought him with his own money, so he's not inclined to share."

"Pity," said the chef. "Where's he from?"

"Gaul. Or is it Germania? One of those. Somewhere north and cold where they breed blonds and redheads," the manager said.

"I see," said the chef.

After his dinner, Gordius had a few drinks with some fellow trainers and gladiators. No longer fighting now he could be more relaxed about how much he ate and drank, but he went back to his room earlier than usual.

Once he was safely out of earshot, one of the trainers commented "Home to the wife."

Another said, "Have you seen him close up? I'd hurry home, too."

And a large African gladiator, who was usually silent said, "And he moves like a gazelle."

The trainers and gladiators exchanged glances.

"All right, Africanus. What's a gazelle?" someone asked.

"A very graceful animal," he said.

When Gordius got back to his room, he found that Marcius had already put out most of the lamps and was dozing in the bed. Marcius, and the room, smelt clean and fresh; and Gordius was pleased with him. He stripped quickly, joined the youth in the bed, and used him quickly before blowing out the last lamps. Although Gordius would sometimes spend the night with a different slave, Marcius slept most nights in Gordius's large comfortable bed, and Gordius started to take Marcius out with him to places in the city such as markets, arenas and theaters. Marcius realized what a huge city Rome was – how rich and how populated.

No wonder we lost, he thought.

Gordius and Marcius soon settled into a routine. Every morning Gordius woke first and would wake Marcius with kisses and caresses. Marcius woke more slowly and smiled sleepily at Gordius. Marcius had no idea how sweet and appealing he looked when he smiled first thing in the morning. Gordius would arouse Marcius by stroking his chest, his belly and reach down to take hold and gently manipulate his penis. Marcius did the same for Gordius. As Marcius was ten years younger than Gordius it did not take Marcius long to achieve a climax. Once Marcius finished satisfying Gordius similarly, he got up, washed and dressed quickly, grabbed his basket from beside the door and went to the kitchens to collect breakfast for himself and Gordius. Gordius relaxed in his bed until Marcius returned with bread, fresh fruit, milk and cheese. Gordius enjoyed a generous, leisurely breakfast shared with Marcius. After breakfast, Gordius went to train new gladiators, and Marcius would do any cleaning and tidying required in Gordius's room. He then went to the kitchen to see if he was required there. Tullius, who managed the kitchens, had discussed Marcius with Gordius, and they had agreed that Marcius could help the other slave boys with their duties in the kitchen and other areas of the arena, but his main duty was to see to Gordius's needs.

"One thing about your lad, Gordius," Tullius said approvingly "He's not lazy."

In the kitchens, Marcius was helpful to Tullius in two ways. He helped cleaning up after breakfast, and he helped translate orders to new kitchen slaves. At that time, thousands of slaves from Gaul were arriving in Rome, and Tullius bought many for working at the arena. They were, after all, young, healthy and cheap. But very few of them knew any Latin. Tullius was a fair and intelligent man. He knew if a new kitchen slave looked at him blankly after being given an order, he was not being disobedient, he simply did not understand.

Marcius not only was almost fluent in Latin, and knew some Greek due to his education, he could also communicate in the dialects spoken in northern Gaul. The dialects spoken in central and southern Gaul were not so easy for him to understand, but the languages were related, and when it came to simple orders, Marcius, with the help of gestures, miming, and the common words, which seemed very similar in various dialects, could help Tullius tell new slaves what he wanted them to do. Most of the new slaves were sensible enough to be grateful for his help, as they had all worked out that a kitchen manager who thinks he is being disobeyed is a kitchen manager who punishes, but some secretly considered Marcius a bit of a crawler.

Marcius usually assisted in the kitchens, but sometimes he was sent with other slave boys to sweep and clean rooms, bathrooms, corridors and attend to torches and lamps. Like the rest of the youths, Marcius preferred these duties as it meant that they were not as closely supervised as when they worked in the kitchens and dining halls. Although they got their work done, there was more time for chatting, gossip and horseplay. It must be admitted that whenever two or three youths were sent to clean the large bathroom favored by the gladiators, a water fight usually resulted with the youths getting more water on themselves than on the actual floor they were supposed to be scrubbing. Luckily, the gladiators found this amusing, as did Tullius.

I can't be everywhere, Tullius told himself. And controlling this lot, some days, is like trying to discipline a swarm of bees.

As they worked and lived together, there was also friendships, alliances, arguments and relationships among the slave boys. Marcius was considered the best looking slave at the arena, but the trainers and gladiators knew he belonged to Gordius, and if they looked at him and admired him, they knew not to touch. But when working with the other lads, some of them flirted with Marcius. Vitas, a slave from Spain, was taller than most of the other lads, wiry and fit. Whenever he and Marcius worked together, he tried to touch, tickle and kiss Marcius. Marcius had to frequently push Vitas away and tell him to stop it. Marcius was attracted to Vitas, too, but he knew that Gordius would get angry with him if he found out.

After being shoved, Vitas would grin at Marcius and say, "One day, Blondie. I'll be as famous a gladiator as Gordius; and then you can be my little princess."

Vitas had a cheeky grin and a casual attitude to anyone in authority. He was frequently caned by Tullius for minor offenses, but Tullius did not want to break Vitas's spirit. Tullius had noticed how agile and fit Vitas was, and thinking about the future, he considered that if Vitas grew a bit taller and put some weight on, he might be worth training as a fighter in a couple of years time. In turn, Vitas accepted being punished by Tullius philosophically.

"That's his job," he said to the other slaves in the slave boys' dormitory at night. "I got worse most days from my crazy old bastard of a father."

Some of the younger lads in the dormitory looked up to Vitas, but Marcius wondered if he was not simply a bit of a thick head.

Gordius did not notice that Vitas flirted with Marcius until he came back to his room a little before midday one day as he had forgotten something. That morning Marcius had been making the bed when Vitas had walked past the open door and come in to help make the bed. Vitas had not intended to help make the bed. He soon grabbed Marcius and started to tickle him. Marcius struggled with Vitas in a half hearted fashion, but he was so ticklish that he could not stop himself laughing. Suddenly, Gordius was in the doorway glaring at them. Vitas immediately let go of Marcius, and removed his hand from under the front of Marcius's tunic, but Gordius knew exactly what was going on.

"Out," he growled at Vitas.

Vitas bolted from the room, ducking and dodging as he ran past Gordius. Gordius stared at Marcius.

Marcius did not think he had seen Gordius so angry before, in fact, he did not think he had seen anyone so coldly angry before.

"Come here, slut," Gordius said.

Marcius made one step forward, then his courage deserted him. Marcius fell to his knees and started to cry. He did not dare look up at Gordius.

"Please master," he begged. "I'm not a slut. You know I'm not. We were just messing about. I haven't done anything with him. I swear that I haven't. He flirts with everyone."

By this time, Gordius had walked towards the kneeling Marcius and was looming over him. Marcius reached out and wrapped a pleading hand around Gordius's massive right lower leg.

"Please master. Don't be too hard on me," Marcius whimpered.

Gordius slapped Marcius's face so hard that Marcius fell onto his side on the floor. Marcius was stunned and brought his hand to his hurt face.

"Not my face, master," he begged. "Don't bruise my face."

Gordius was angry and determined to punish Marcius, but he was still thinking rationally. He knew how easy it would be for a man of his strength to seriously injure a delicate youth like Marcius. So he picked him up, dragged him over to the bed and sat down. He hauled Marcius over his lap. He quickly lifted up Marcius's tunic and pulled his loincloth down and off. He then started to beat Marcius's bare buttocks. Marcius had always known that Gordius was strong; he had no idea how strong until a series of blows descended on his bare flesh. Marcius cried out with each swat, but he did not struggle or protest. He had learned when Simonides had punished him that if he resisted, protested or tried to get away, it would only result in a harder, more prolonged beating. The slaps seemed to go on for a long time. Gordius only decided that he had punished Marcius enough when Marcius was lying limp across his thighs, crying and whimpering pathetically. Gordius let Marcius up from his position across his lap, and Marcius fell onto his knees on the floor.

"Sorry, master. I'm sorry, master," he whispered as his hands went to rub his now crimson red bottom. As Gordius looked at Marcius weeping and rubbing his sore bottom, it occurred to him how boyish, miserable and piteous Marcius looked. He also realized just how much he loved him. Gordius picked Marcius up from the floor and carried Marcius to his side of their bed. He placed him gently on his stomach on the bed. Gordius lay on the other side of the bed and let Marcius cry into his pillow. He stroked his upper back gently as he did so.

"It's all over now, little Marcius. It's all finished. I'm not angry with you anymore," Gordius said.

Gordius let Marcius stay in bed the next day. He went to have his breakfast with the other trainers, but he said very little during the meal. The slaves who served the meal tip toed around Gordius nervously. One or two trainers grinned at each other as if to say: Lovers' quarrel. They'll get over it.

Tullius beckoned Gordius to his office after breakfast.

"Do you want me to punish Vitas?" he asked Gordius.

"How do you know?" Marcius asked.

"Working here is like living in a very small village. No one has any secrets. Beside, Vitas came to my office. He was frightened that you were going to injure Marcius. I hope you weren't too hard on him, Gordius. Vital would have started it."

"How do you know?" Gordius asked.

"Because he always does. He's a nuisance that way. Some of the boys complain to me."

"But not Marcius?"

"No. That means nothing, Gordius. Your Marcius has a kind heart, and he would not like to see Vitas caned for a bit of fooling about. Be fair, Gordius. Weren't you ever randy and foolish when you were a kid?"

"I never was a kid. I was fighting Roman soldiers when I was fourteen."

"Fourteen?"

"I was big for my age," Gordius said.

"I can imagine that," Tullius said. "I told Vitas to leave your lad alone, or I would hand him over to you for a proper whipping in front of the other lads. I think he'll take notice. There's plenty of other boys he likes, and who fancy him."

The next day, Marcius went back to work in the kitchens. The other kitchen slaves assumed that he had been severely whipped by Gordius and were sympathetic. Marcius did not like to admit that Gordius had taken him over his lap, bared his bottom, and spanked him as if he was a small child. The whole procedure might not have been as painful as a whipping, but it was more humiliating.

For the next few days, Marcius went about his duties but he barely spoke to Gordius. After three days of this, after dinner Gordius made Marcius sit on his lap and cuddled him.

"Aren't you ever going to forgive me, little Gaul?" he asked.

"It's not that, master. I don't want to annoy you. My bum is just beginning to feel normal again," Marcius said.

"I have slapped you before, Marcius," Gordius said.

"But not as hard as that," Marcius said. "And, before, well, I did ... sort of ... ask for it."

Marcius was correct. Soon after being bought by Gordius, Marcius had said something cheeky to him, downright insolent in fact. Marcius had been testing the huge gladiator, pushing the limits, seeing how much he could get away with. Gordius had grinned, but then he grabbed Marcius, bent him over his table, held his still and administered some hard smacks to his bottom. Marcius burst into tears, and Gordius stopped hitting him. He put his arms around him and hugged him while Marcius composed himself. Then he looked at him seriously and said, "Little Gaul. You're a slave now. One day you'll be a freed slave. But you can't talk to someone who owns you like that. A Roman owner would really hurt you for being insolence. They don't tolerate it. If you don't learn that now, you won't survive."

Before Gordius punished Marcius over his behaviour with Vitas, Gordius had chastised Marcius on a few occasions usually for answering back. But he had not lost his temper on those occasions, and he considered that he was trying to be fair to Marcius, and that for his own sake, Marcius had to learn to think carefully before he expressed his opinions to someone who was his master. Marcius did forgive Gordius, but he also became more careful about what he said and did.

In winter, Gordius realized just how much Marcius felt the cold. Marcius found more covers for Gordius's bed and kept a fire going in the brazier in the room for hours, but some nights, when Gordius got into bed, he found Marcius's hands and feet quite cold. Considering that Marcius was from the north of Gaul, he was surprised that Marcius was not more used to cold weather. Then he told himself: He's thin, and often ill. I bet his mum never let him outside their round house without making sure he was wearing layers of clothes.

So, Gordius took Marcius to a market where a lively trade in second hand clothes went on. Gordius had his tunics made by a tailor, but this was nothing to do with vanity. Gordius only required that his tunics be plain and comfortable, but due to his height and width, a tailor needed to measure him correctly to make something large enough. Gordius thought he might find some warm clothing for Marcius among the second hand goods on sale. Tullius recommended a trader called Andronica to Gordius. Andronica bought garments from Rome's fashionable ladies and youths who liked to keep up with the latest trends. As a result, her garments were good quality, in fact, some had hardly been worn. She had a sister who owned a laundry, so her garments were spotlessly clean when sold. Andronica also employed her daughters and granddaughters in making any minor repairs to these garments before sale.

They complained about this, but she told her family, "When you're ladies of leisure, you can sit around, and do pretty embroidery. Until then, we have a living to make, so get busy on those hems."

When Gordius walked over to her stall, she wondered vaguely just how much material it would take to make a tunic for Gordius. So she was relieved when he said, “I want something warm for my lad. He feels the cold.”

Andronica looked at the slightly built fair youth standing behind Gordius.

Now that’s what I call a sweet looking boy, she thought. Even if his clothes are very old and tatty.

“No wonder he feels the cold, sir,” she said. “There’s no flesh on him to keep him warm. Not like some of us.”

Gordius grinned. Not only was he exceptionally tall, perhaps, the tallest man in Rome, he was also very solid. Andronica was no delicate maiden herself, in fact, if a sculptor wandered past while wondering where he could find a model for a fertility goddess, he would have immediately offered Andronica the job. Andronica persuaded Gordius to buy for Marcius a linen under tunic, a plain light colored woolen tunic, which was suitable to be worn as an under tunic in winter or a tunic in summer, and a thicker well made woolen tunic dyed a reddish brown colour. They discussed a cloak for Marcius. Andronica persuaded Gordius that a long, wide dark gray woolen clock with a hood would be best for Marcius. Gordius paid for the tunics and cloak. Andronica rolled them and put them in Marcius’s basket. Marcius put on the cloak and was pleased and surprised just how comfortable and warm the garment was. Andronica then had another thought.

“How about some breeches?” she asked.

“Romans don’t wear breeches,” said Gordius.

“But I’m not a Roman, master,” Marcius said. “And I’ve seen Roman soldiers who wore breeches, especially cavalry officers. Think of the problems they’d have with chaffing if they didn’t.”

A couple of legionaries standing near Gordius and Marcius laughed at Marcius's comments.

"Now I know why cavalry officers are such shits. The chaffing is killing them," he whispered to his friend.

"Here," said Andronica as she rolled up the breaches and put them in the basket. "No extra charge. If you're looking for boots for him, my brother's store is just across the way, next to the tavern. Mention my name; he'll give you a good price."

It took a while for the cobbler to find some short boots for Marcius as he had such small, if slender, feet. As Gordius walked back to the arena with Marcius, he knew that he had spent more than he had intended, but Marcius was obviously so pleased with his new clothes and grateful for them when the weather was really cold, that Gordius realized that his money was well spent. And when Marcius unrolled the contents of his basket, he was surprised to find two pairs of socks wrapped in the trousers, which he was sure Gordius had not bought.

In the middle of winter, on very cold days, when Marcius ran an errand for Gordius or another trainer, he wore his tunics, trousers, cloak, socks and boots and was better dressed than most of Rome's poor free citizens. Because of his long blond hair and trousers, many people assumed that he was the son of a prosperous merchant or trader from somewhere north, until they noticed his slave tag. Shabbily dressed free born youths who envied his clothes, muttered to each other, "It's better to be poor than some rich bastard's cup bearer."

Marcius had been stunned when Gordius told him he should wear a slave tag. He looked at Gordius with a hurt look on his face.

"But you know that I would never run away from you, master. You're good to me; I would not be ungrateful like that."

"I don't mean it as a punishment, Marcius. But I've seen how men stare at you and follow you even when you're with me. No one will bother you as soon as they see a tag saying you belong to me. Only a very brave or very stupid man would annoy a big, ugly, vicious gladiator like me by molesting my slave."

"But you're not like that, master. You're big, but you're not ugly or vicious," Marcius said.

"That's our little secret, little Gaul. My reputation will protect you," Gordius said.

So Marcius wore a slave collar with a tag engraved with the words: "Marcius, slave of Gordius the Thracian, Trainer, Statilii Tauri Amphitheatre."

He was not bothered much afterwards as he went on his errands. Older men who would have approached him assumed that such a beautiful, well groomed and well dressed slave must belong to someone very rich and powerful. Marcius only really was bothered by soldiers, sailors or gladiators coming out of the taverns in the late afternoon who somewhat optimistically assumed he was a prostitute. Marcius soon learned to say quickly and politely, "Excuse me, sir. My master, Gordius the gladiator, is waiting for me at the arena."

Everyone seemed to have heard of Gordius, and Marcius could return to the arena with no further trouble.

One evening, as Gordius was undressing before bed, Marcius asked him, "Why are people so frightened of you, master?"

"Did something happen at the market?" Gordius asked.

"Nothing important. Just a big centurion tried to chat me up, but as soon as I said your name, and he looked at my tag, he looked, well, worried."

Gordius grinned.

"I have a certain reputation," Gordius said. "A couple of years ago, just before I retired I won a series of fights against tough opponents. Many people came to see those fights. Some people still talk about them. I won enough prize money to buy my freedom from Antonius. I could have kept fighting for a couple more years and won more perhaps, but I decided to become a trainer. I'm a good trainer. I know when a lad has talent. But I was one of the best when I was fighting."

"But you just like a big puppy dog really," Marcius commented.

Gordius burst out laughing and said, "Puppy dog, am I? I'll show you big puppy dog, cheeky boy".

Gordius pulled down the covers and fell onto the bed. He grabbed Marcius and started to tickle him. He tickled Marcius who squirmed and laughed until Marcius said, "Please. Enough."

Gordius knew this was childish, but he liked to see Marcius smile, and he liked to make him laugh. At the end of their play wrestle and tickle, both Marcius and Gordius were aroused. Gordius whispered in Marcius's ear, "Do you want to roll over for me, lovely boy. Only if you want to."

Marcius smiled invitingly at Gordius.

"Yes, master. I want to," Marcius said.

As Marcius rolled onto his stomach, positioned himself and spread his legs, Gordius found a small jar of lubricating ointment under the bed. Marcius was used to letting Gordius use him like this now. Gordius always applied plenty of lubricant to Marcius and himself, he always tried to be gentle, and not hurt the youth he loved. And if Marcius sometimes enjoyed this more times than others, he wanted to please and satisfy Gordius sexually. He wanted to show Gordius that he appreciated his kindness and that he loved him.

Later Marcius said to Gordius, "I'm glad you don't fight in the arena any more, master."

"Would you watch me if I did?" Gordius asked.

"Not unless you told me I had to. I know you can fight; I've seen you training the new fighters. I know how skilled you are, but I would not like to see you kill someone or be killed."

In fact, unlike everyone else who lived and worked in the arena, Marcius tried to avoid watching the fights for the public. All the other slave boys found them exciting and looked forward to them. In fact, Tullius used confining a slave boy to the boys' dormitory on these days quite an effective punishment. Gordius, of course, watched the fighters he trained compete. But he still enjoyed a fair fight between well matched opponents. He found Marcius's attitude hard to understand.

"But you're from Gaul, Marcius. Isn't hunting and fighting what your people do best?" he asked.

"We hunt and fight when it's a matter of survival and honor: we don't murder each other for the amusement of an idle, ignorant mob," Marcius said.

"Shush, Marcius. That's dangerous talk," Gordius said, but he knew what Marcius was talking about.

One night Gordius took Marcius to a dinner party at a genuine mansion. The host, Julius Porcius Atellus was rich, dissolute, ugly enough to be repulsive and had a reputation for cruelty. (In a society which knew all about cruelty!). Gordius always enjoyed Atellus's parties and wondered what all the fuss was about. Admittedly, Gordius met there mainly rich freedmen and their wives, gladiators, actors, expensive prostitutes and a few young friends of Atellus; but there was plenty of good food and wine, talk, jokes and entertainment. This night, Gordius enjoyed the openly admiring looks at Marcius from the other guests. One freedwoman, Flavia, who owned to Gordius's knowledge at least six of the best brothels in Rome, asked loudly after a few cups of wine.

"How much for your blond? He could make me a fortune. I could retire!" she said.

Gordius laughed and said; "He's not for sale."

"He should be," Flavia suggested.

Marcius felt his face getting warmer and realized that he was blushing. Flavia roared with laughter and nudged her near neighbor Claudia. Claudia and Flavia had been each other's major business rival for so many years that they had ended up as best friends.

"Look at that. And he's sweet, too," she commented.

She let the topic drop, but she decided to remember Gordius's slave from Gaul. Marcius did not mind Flavia looking at him, but he did not like the way Atellus glanced at him. Atellus looked peeved. Atellus was thinking how did I miss that one? And how did a gladiator afford him?

For Atellus was a collector of beautiful slaves. He was so ugly himself that people who disliked him (that is, most people) joked that his mother must have been frightened by a crocodile in Egypt when expecting him. But Atellus was born with an artist's passion for beauty. He wrote, painted and sculpted with real ability, but because he set himself such high standards he was always disappointed with what he produced. As an alternative, he collected beautiful objects and slaves. But, he was bitter. Rumor had it that he took out his bitterness on the beautiful slaves he bought, but he was so rich he could pay fantastic prices for them, so slave dealers ignored the rumors. A Greek youth lay beside Atellus that evening. As he was an actor and dancer, he had entertained his master's guests, but he did not say very much during the meal. It was just as well that he was sitting next to Flavia who could chat about nothing in particular for hours.

However, she said to Claudia at they shared a litter to their respective homes that evening, “Atellus has that Greek boy frightened.”

“Atellus could frighten anyone,” said Claudia. “He had his eye on Gordius’s lad.”

“I noticed,” said Flavia.

“So did you,” Claudia said.

“In a professional capacity,” said Flavia.

“Oh come on,” said Claudia. “We’re not that old!”

“Is it just me or are young men better looking than when we were young?” Flavia asked.

“I’ve noticed that, too,” said Claudia. “It could be because we spent our youth with older men.”

“Who were often very sweet,” Flavia said.

“And very generous,” Claudia said.

Both Flavia and Claudia had been promoted by generous benefactors to run brothels they later bought. And to the best of their abilities they both protected their boys and girls.

“I would not like to see it,” Flavia said.

“What?” said Claudia.

“That fair boy with Atellus. The Greek looks like he knows the score. Not that lad from Gaul.”

“Do you think he’s as innocent as he looks?” Claudia asked.

“Possibly. He did blush when I teased him,” Flavia said.

“He could have been faking,” Claudia suggested.

“As you and I know, Claudia, many things can be faked. But I don’t know if blushing is one of them.”

Gordius and Marcius spent the night in one of Atellus's guest rooms as there were plenty of them. But Marcius did not sleep well. He disliked the house's atmosphere, and he woke once during the night sure that he had heard someone weeping somewhere.

A few weeks later, everything changed for Marcius. During training, Gordius was showing a gladiator a better way of defending himself when he was hit in the back by a javelin. It was a simple accident. A trainee gladiator had thrown a spear with great force and enthusiasm but little sense of direction. Gordius was dying as he hit the ground. His huge body was lifted by gladiators and carried to the surgeon's infirmary but there was nothing he could do. Marcius ran from the kitchen as soon as he heard someone say Gordius was hurt. He arrived in time to take Gordius's hand, and he smiled at.

"Little Marcius. You have to survive," Gordius gasped as he struggled to breathe. "You're young. You have time to earn you freedom. You can do it and go home to your people. If you do that, they captured you, but they did not defeat you."

The surgeon and Antonius kept everyone else out as the gigantic man and slim youth said good bye. They kissed for the last time.

Antonius kept the grieving Marcius with him for a few days. They both faced an uncertain future. Antonius managed a few fighters, but he had also relied on a percentage of Gordius's income. Now, he needed to find more fighters to manage. He felt too old to start again, but he had no choice. He decided that he could sell Marcius to Tullius. Marcius could continue working in the kitchens with the other slaves.

CHAPTER 3

Atellus, who heard of Gordius's death very quickly, sent an offer for Marcius. The sum suggested was five times what Gordius had paid for him. Antonius began to dream of a new business venture. For years he had been thinking of buying a share in a friend's small tavern in the south on the seaside.

Atellus might not be so bad, Antonius told himself. People say all sorts of things about rich people they dislike.

The surgeon tried reason and Marcius begged, but Marcius was sold to Atellus anyway. Antonius paid a gladiator to chain and escort Marcius to Atellus's mansion. Despite the awful penalties, Marcius thought for the first time about running away. But where would he go and who would help him? And he knew Atellus would do something terrible to him if he tried to escape, so he followed meekly like someone resigned to being executed. Calcus the butler opened the door and leered at his master's new slave. If there was a competition for most evil looking man in Rome, Atellus and his favorite servant would come a very close first and second. (And some serious money would have been bet on Calcus).

Calcus grabbed Marcius's upper arm firmly and lead him through the kitchen. Marcius had expected this. He was used to kitchens and slave quarters near kitchens. But Calcus opened a large door and took the boy downstairs to a cellar. There were large jars, boxes and crates. At the foot of the stairs, without letting go of Marcius's arm, Calcus stooped to pick something up. Marcius saw that it was a cane. Calcus lead Marcius to a corner where there was some straw, blankets, a chain and collar attached to the wall.

"Guard dog?" Marcius wondered.

Then he noticed the lidded bucket. He realized the corner was meant for him. He had been told that all things were bigger and better in Rome, but he did not seriously think that the Romans had trained their dogs to use buckets for sanitary purposes. (Now that he really would consider civilized). Calcus switched Marcius's legs and locked the iron collar around his neck.

"Now," he said as he switched Marcius again. "Stay quiet down here. Your master will send for you this evening and explain the rules. If I hear a sound from you until then, I'll use this cane on that sweet little bottom of yours. Understood?"

Marcius nodded. He sat down miserably on the straw and pulled the blankets around him.

A blond one for a change, thought Calcus. But, I'm not sure he's worth what the master paid for him. Still, it's not my money.

That evening, Marcius was unchained and escorted upstairs. Calcus was surprised to see that Marcius seemed calm. He was used to them being terrified by this stage, but Marcius seemed to have gone beyond that. Atellus waited for him sitting on a chair in his bedroom. He was wearing a light colored tunic, which looked comfortable.

"Come here, slave," he said.

He ordered Marcius to strip, but he did not touch him yet. He ordered Marcius to turn around slowly a couple of times.

As beautiful as a Greek statue, Atellus thought. He's shorter than even an average Roman youth, but he's perfectly proportioned. Even his hands and feet are small and slender.

Atellus pointed to a piece of furniture in a corner of the room.

"What is that?" he asked.

“It’s a cupboard,” Marcius said.

“In front of that?” Atellus asked impatiently.

“A table. No, it’s too low. A footstool?” Marcius suggested.

“Well done. You look stupid but you’re not,” Atellus said.

Atellus took the boy by his wrist and took him to the footstool. Atellus opened the cupboard. Marcius had expected to see clothes. Instead, he saw a range of implements on a neat row of little hooks. There were whips, canes, straps and a birch rod. They were all to do with inflicting pain.

Is there anything this man does not collect? Marcius asked himself.

“Which do you think I should use on you first?” Atellus asked.

“Have I done something wrong, master?” Marcius asked fearfully. Marcius could not imagine how he had managed to displease his new master in such a short time.

“You have not done anything wrong, and after the lesson I’m going to give you, you will never dare disobey me or displease me. I’m going to teach you respect,” Atellus said. “I think perhaps the rod since you’re a barbarian. You’ll be used to that.”

Marcius did not know what to say for a moment.

“Please master,” he begged. “Don’t birch me. I’ve been taught. My masters before … they punished me ... I know how to be obedient, how to be quiet, how to please you. Please, master, give me a chance to be a good slave, a pleasing slave.”

Marcius was looking up into his new master’s face with tears in his eyes.

He really is lovely, Atellus thought. It's not just because he is so fair and has perfect features, it's because he looks so sweet, sincere and innocent when he's frightened and begs for mercy.

"Kneel down and bend over the stool," Atellus ordered.

Marcius did so quickly hoping that if he was submissive and obeyed his master immediately this might prove that he knew how to obey, and his new master would not be too harsh with him. Atellus did understand why Marcius so quickly obeyed him.

He knows if he does not obey an order instantly he will be punished more severely. Someone has taught this pretty little animal that, Atellus thought.

Atellus tied the boy's wrists and legs into position but he did not gag him. He wanted to hear Marcius's screams and cries. When he gave his new boy this first thrashing, he expected a good deal of screaming, struggling and crying. But before he began to whip Marcius, he leaned over, pushed his long blond hair aside, and whispered into his ear, "Scream as much as you like. I like to hear a bitch scream. I'll make you scream."

He was not disappointed at Marcius's first loud anguished screams as his master's birch rod hit Marcius's buttocks. Atellus had decided not to count the number of strokes he would give Marcius. He beat Marcius from one side giving him about twenty hard cuts across his buttocks as Marcius cried out in pain. Simonides had strapped him and Gordius had slapped him, but Marcius had never been birched or whipped before by a strong man intent on hurting him so much. Then Atellus stopped beating Marcius and changed position, so he could beat him from the other side.

Marcius thought the pause meant his master had finished beating him, so he cried out, "Please master. No more, I'll be a good slave, a good boy, a good bitch, please, no more!"

"I have barely started with you," Atellus sneered.

The stripes criss-crossed across Marcius's buttocks by the time Atellus decided he had beaten him enough. He put the rod back in the cupboard. He knelt behind Marcius and parted his cheeks. He was pleased that he was still conscious. Atellus was surprised that he really had to force his large penis inside Marcius.

When he had first seen Marcius, Atellus had thought: That one pretends he's not a slut, and he looks so sweet, but how can he keep that big fit gladiator satisfied if he isn't a slut.

Atellus tried not to move too fast as he was enjoying himself in such a tight little hole, and he also wanted to hurt Marcius and prolong his torment as long as possible. And Marcius did feel all the pain of it. It was more painful than his first time with the Roman soldier as the soldier had not beaten him first.

Atellus untied the sobbing youth and dragged him to the foot of his bed. He dumped him on the floor there. He threw a blanket over him.

"You sleep there like the filthy little animal you are. You'll sleep in the bed with me if I decide you deserve to," he said.

Atellus went to sleep with a smug, satisfied look on his face. Marcius lay on the cold floor and wept quietly. Admittedly, he had been beaten before but never like Atellus had beaten him. He had begged pathetically. He knew that this was what Atellus wanted, and he was frightened that he would beat him to death if he did not beg for mercy. Marcius thought about Simonides the slave trader who had strapped him to teach him a lesson. Marcius had learned that lesson to some extent. But this was different. He knew that Atellus was not trying to teach him anything, he had birched Marcius for the sheer sadistic pleasure of it. And Gordius? Gordius had spanked him sometimes for flirting or being cheeky. Afterwards, Gordius usually kissed, petted and comforted the weeping youth.

Marcius was woken by Atellus saying loudly, "Wake up and come here, slave."

Marcius dragged his cold, aching body up from the floor and got into his master's bed. He lay on his side and looked at Atellus waiting for his next order. Atellus pushed Marcius's long fair hair away from his face.

"Good. I haven't killed you. That would be a terrible waste of my money. Do you know why I birched you like that?"

Marcius did not know what the safe answer was so he said, "No master."

"Did you deserve it?" Atellus asked.

"If you say so, master," Marcius said.

"It's so you know what to expect if you don't please me. Now, suck me."

"Please master. It hurts to move," Marcius whimpered.

Atellus smiled coldly.

"In that case, I'll fuck your bottom again," Atellus said.

Marcius started to beg, "No, master. Please, don't do that. Please!"

"You really are stupid," Atellus said as he sat up. He reached over and turned Marcius onto his stomach. With his left hand on the small of Marcius's back he held him in position as he started to administer as series of hard smacks to Marcius's lacerated bottom with his right hand. Normally, a spanking would not have been so unbearable, but Marcius was already in such pain that he could barely move. He cringed under the blows and begged for mercy.

"Please ... please master. Please ... I'm sorry ... Please stop ... I'll do anything ... I'll please you ... Please ..."

The slaps continued. Desperately, Marcius reached his hand out for his master's penis to caress and arouse him. He hoped that if he excited him the punishment would stop. Atellus long, thick penis was soon fully erect in Marcius's hand.

"Please ... fuck me," Marcius begged.

"That's better," Atellus said and he stopped slapping him. Marcius spread his legs as much as he could without being told to. Atellus positioned himself between Marcius's spread legs and grabbed his hips pulling Marcius's bottom closer to him. Without using any lubricant, he pushed inside Marcius and started thrusting vigorously. Marcius screamed once in anguish, and moaned and whimpered as Atellus thrust inside him.

"I'm going to make you bleed, bitch," Atellus hissed in Marcius's ear.

Atellus climaxed with a loud groan then withdrew. Sweating and panting Atellus rolled back on his side of the bed. Once he had his breathe back, he stood up and walked to his bedroom door. He opened the door and called out.

"Calcus! You can come and get him now."

Atellus returned to his bed and fell asleep. Calcus appeared quickly and dragged Marcius from the bed. He picked up Marcius's clothes from the floor and half carried the naked youth from the room.

"You smell like a whore," he sneered as he took him to the slaves' bathroom.

The warm water did help ease Marcius's pain but Calcus frightened him when he said, "Wash yourself thoroughly or I'll do it for you. The master likes a clean pretty bitch."

Once he was dry, Marcius was taken back to the cellar by Calcus. He fell onto the straw and blankets exhausted. He barely noticed as Calcus chained him by the neck again. Hours later, he woke to find Calcus dabbing some stinging liquid on his stripes and he yelped.

"Stay still, bitch," Calcus warned. "This is for your own good. Master doesn't want your cuts infected."

Calcus finished his task and started up the stairs. He looked at Marcius in his corner once briefly. With grim satisfaction he said, "You're not so pretty now, little Gaul."

A few hours later, Marcius woke up and realized that it was nearly dusk. One of the household slaves, Cleon, was looking at him. He had a bowl containing some food and a small ceramic jug. He put it down in front of Marcius.

"I don't want it," Marcius said.

Cleon looked at the stairs anxiously.

"Aren't you allowed to speak to me?" Marcius asked.

"Not really," Cleon whispered. "But you have to eat. Calcus will cane you if you don't eat or make yourself sick."

"I see," said Marcius.

Marcius was thirsty if not hungry, so he grabbed the jug and took a sip. To his surprise the wine was not watered down.

"I expected that to be water," Marcius said.

"Master's orders. He said that's how you people prefer your wine," Cleon explained.

"But why should he do that?" Marcius asked.

"That's how he works. Punishments and rewards. If you obey them then you'll get enough food, drink, and blankets. If you disobey, Calcus takes them away and they beat you," Cleon said.

"How long have you been here?" Marcius asked.

"Three months," Cleon said.

Marcius suddenly knew who he was; the Greek boy who had danced at the dinner party. But he looked different now. Marcius also realized that the boy was risking a caning by talking to him and was trying to help him.

"Thanks," he said.

Marcius ate the cheese, olives and bread that Cleon had brought down to him. As he finished, he handed the plate to Cleon.

"Don't give up, Marcius. He won't keep you for more than a couple of months. He gets bored quickly. Then he'll sell you," Cleon said.

"Who to?" Marcius asked.

"Does it matter?" Cleon asked cynically.

"But he's kept you longer," Marcius said.

"He still fucks me sometimes. I'm a dancer and acrobat. He likes the positions I can get into. And I entertain his guests. Besides, he's given me to Calcus now, and Calcus isn't tired of me yet," Cleon said.

"How am I going to survive two or three months?" Marcius asked.

"The beatings won't be so severe from now on," Cleon said.

"Why not?" Marcius asked.

"Soon he'll give you to his friends," Cleon said.

"What?" said Marcius.

"You are new to Rome," Cleon commented. "He has dinner parties most nights, and slaves like you and me serve the food and wine at his parties, and please his friends afterwards. They don't hurt us. He doesn't allow that. We don't belong to them. The master won't ruin your looks. Your skin is so fair that your bruises and stripes will look awful, and he won't like his friends to see that. He'll bully you to keep you in line, but the beatings won't be so bad," Cleon said.

"How do you know all this?" Marcius asked.

Cleon shrugged and said, "He's done it to me, and Calcus tells me things. Calcus talks more than the master, and I belong to Calcus now. I'm sorry, Marcius. I have to go now."

Marcius was left chained in the cellar for a couple of days and nights. But Cleon brought him food and water three times a day, spoke to him as much as he could, and continued to empty and clean the bucket once a day. Cleon even managed to beg from Calcus a lamp for Marcius, so he could have some light in the evenings. Much of the time, Marcius slept.

Calcus unchained him and escorted him to have a bath every day. Marcius did not much like the way Calcus looked at him lustfully as he bathed, but there was nothing he could do about it. He wondered how long it would be before Calcus would be given permission to use him.

On the third morning, Calcus watched Marcius bathe as usual, but when he got out of the bath instead of just handing him the towel he held it open and said, "Come here, pretty. I'm going to dry you."

When Marcius hesitated, Calcus frowned and reached for the cane, which he had briefly put down. Marcius went to him quickly.

"No, please sir. I'll do anything you say," Marcius said.

Calcus looked at the stripes on Marcius's back, buttocks and the backs of his thighs. They were still ugly, but healing.

Calcus ran the palm of his right hand over Marcius's bottom. Marcius tensed but he did not move or say anything.

"Are you still sore?" Calcus asked.

"A little, sir," Marcius said.

"Don't worry, slut. You're healing. Your bum will be as pretty as it was; as long as you don't anger your master tonight."

"Yes, sir," Marcius said. "I understand."

Calcus took his time drying and fondling Marcius. He paid particular attention to his bottom, nipples and genitals. Calcus felt his own penis begin to stiffen. In fact, he was tempted to bend the youth over then and there, or at least, make him get on his knees and suck.

But not yet, Calcus thought. The master would not like it. I'll get my turn soon enough. Atellus won't keep this one long. He's the prettiest in a long time, but he's no real challenge. He likes to break their spirit, but this one's spirit was broken long ago. The master will tire of him soon. And in the meantime, I can have Cleon any time I like.

Impatiently, he hurried Marcius into his clothes, took him to the cellar and chained him. Quickly, Calcus went in search of Cleon. Cleon was in the kitchen cutting up some vegetables for the chef, Lucretius. Calcus looked at Cleon lustfully. Atellus had actually legally given Cleon to Calcus and he was a valuable gift. If not as lovely as Marcius, he was still a beautiful youth with all the sexual expertise that Marcius lacked. For Cleon had been born and bred in a Greek brothel. Calcus had decided that he would sell Cleon to a Roman brothel one day, and he expected to make quite a profit.

"Come with me, Cleon," he ordered.

Lucretius protested, "Hell, Calcus. He has work to do. I need his help."

"I'll send him back as soon as I've finished," Calcus said.

"See you in three minutes, Cleon," Lucretius said.

Calcus ignored the insult as Lucretius was the only slave in the household over whom he had no power. This chef was one of the best in Rome, and he knew it. When he had first arrived Calcus had tried to assert his authority by hitting Lucretius across the back with his cane. Lucretius was a big man, like most chefs, and he wrestled the cane from Calcus, broke it into two pieces and attempted to insert the two pieces into a certain part of Calcus's anatomy. The only thing that prevented him doing so was Atellus's arrival at the kitchen doorway and the threat of a genuine flogging. He could ignore a freedman like Calcus, but not his owner. When Calcus had demanded that Atellus punish Lucretius, Atellus laughed and said, "He's the best chef in Rome; you are not the best butler. He cost me ten times what you did. Besides, who told you to flog my chef? Your job is to keep my pretty boys in line."

"My authority in this house," Calcus started to say.

"Your authority! You don't have any authority except what I give you. Leave my chef alone or I'll give you fifty lashes. I might have freed you, Calcus, but if I turn you out of this house, you'll starve."

An uneasy truce had existed ever since that incident.

In Calcus's room, he stripped Cleon quickly. Cleon smiled sensuously as if he was enjoying this. Calcus knew that Cleon was acting, but he did not care. He knew that Cleon feared him as much as Marcius did, but Cleon was a whore and could fake practically anything. If anything, he admired Cleon's professionalism. Calcus stripped quickly and positioned himself on the bed.

"Get on with it, bitch," he said.

Cleon knelt and began to suck expertly as he always did.

"You love it, don't you, bitch?" Calcus whispered.

"Yes, master," Cleon said. "I love sucking you. I love your taste."

"Lying whore," Calcus said but, if anything, he meant it as a compliment.

"Enough," Calcus said. "Get on the bed,"

Cleon immediately stood up, then lay on the bed on his belly. Cleon quickly pulled up his tunic, pulled down his loincloth, and positioned his body so that his bottom was raised. Calcus enthusiastically grabbed Cleon's body by his slim hips and pulled him close to him. Within seconds, he had lifted his own tunic, entered Cleon's bottom and started to enjoy his rapid thrusts inside him. Calcus climaxed with an ecstatic groan. Then he stood up, readjusted his clothes, gave Cleon a hard slap to his buttocks and said, "Get back to work, bitch."

Cleon wiped himself with the sheet, readjusted his clothes and returned to his work in the kitchen.

"Not quite three minutes," said Lucretius. "But close enough."

Still, it amazed Lucretius how detached Cleon was about how Calcus used and treated him.

"Are you all right?" he asked.

Cleon shrugged.

"It's nothing," he said. "I don't think about it. He didn't beat me. That's all that matters."

CHAPTER 4

One afternoon, as ordered, Cleon brought to Marcius in the cellar a white linen tunic, sandals and a hairbrush. Calcus had already unchained him. Marcius unbound his braided hair, and carefully brushed it. Then he put on the sandals and tunic. Once Marcius was dressed, Cleon realized the effect that Atellus wanted.

There's a myth, isn't there? Cleon thought. About Zeus abducting an innocent, sweet shepherd. Dressed like that and with his hair loose, Marcius looks like a shepherd boy, Cleon thought, or a sheep about to be sacrificed.

"What's he going to do?" Marcius asked him.

"You are going to dine with him in the main dining room; just the two of you," Cleon explained.

"What does that mean?" Marcius asked.

"I'm not sure. But if he acts affectionately, kissing, touching, cuddling, don't be affectionate back. It's a trick. I fell for that one, and he punished me for being a liar," Cleon said.

"What do I do then?" Marcius asked.

"Do everything his says. Submit to everything he does. Accept it, but don't reciprocate. Be humble and obedient. Act as if you're frightened the whole time," Cleon advised.

"Act as if I'm frightened?" Marcius asked. "I think I can do that, Cleon. I'm terrified of him!"

"Well, that's the safest way," Cleon said. "Oh and no loincloth."

"What?"

“His orders. He might fuck you on the couch. He gets randy after a few cups of wine,” Cleon said.

“But ...” Marcius said.

“What does it matter? You’re not going to leave the house. Just be grateful that it’s a warm day,” Cleon said.

As Calcus escorted Marcius to the dining room even he had to admire how fresh, young and innocent Marcius looked.

The master certainly has an eye for this sort of thing, he told himself.

So Marcius dined with Atellus. Marcius had not gone hungry in Atellus’s household, but the food eaten by his household slaves were simple foods like bread, milk, cheese, grains, fruits and vegetables. Marcius was from a family of hunters and farmers and was used to meat as part of his diet. There were some fish and meat dishes on Atellus’s table that night. Atellus observed that Marcius ate as if he appreciated the dishes, but his table manners were good.

This lad is no peasant’s son, Atellus thought.

Cleon served the meal and poured wine into cups for both of them. Atellus drank his wine warmed with water, but Marcius drank his wine without added water.

“Have you had enough to eat, Marcius?” Atellus asked after a time.

“Yes master,” Marcius said.

“Did you enjoy it?”

“Yes, thank you, master,”

“Better than the food you get in the cellar?” Atellus asked.

"There's nothing wrong with the food I get when I'm in the cellar," Marcius replied cautiously. "I like most food. I'm grateful for what you give me, master."

"Why are you grateful, boy?" Atellus asked.

"I don't do anything to earn it. I don't do any work here," Marcius said.

Atellus laughed and reached over and under Marcius's tunic to caress him.

"I didn't buy you for work. You're a weakling. I can't imagine you in a field. You'd be dead in a few weeks," Atellus said.

"I know, master, but I can work in a household. I have been taught to clean. I could do that if you wanted me to, master."

"I have enough household slaves. I keep you because you're pretty like a painted vase or statue or mosaic. Besides, you have your uses. Come closer to me," Atellus said.

Atellus was lying on his side and pulled Marcius closer to him. Then he kissed his face, neck and mouth. Marcius closed his eyes but otherwise did not respond.

"You hated that, didn't you? Being kissed by me. Because I'm so ugly, so repulsive," Atellus asked.

Marcius said nothing.

"Answer me, bitch." Atellus said.

Marcius opened his eyes. "You're not repulsive, master. I'm frightened of you, that's all," Marcius said.

"So you don't think I'm ugly?" Atellus asked.

"It doesn't matter what I think," Marcius said.

"Why not?" Atellus asked.

"I'm nothing, nobody. A weakling, a coward. Your slave. You can do anything you like to me. It doesn't matter what I think about anything."

"You're not as stupid as I thought. You're beginning to learn your place," Atellus said.

Atellus turned Marcius onto his side with his back to him, lifted the back of his tunic and started to rub himself against the youth's buttocks. Then, to Marcius's surprise, he reached over to fondle him. Marcius could not help becoming aroused.

"You hate me. I repulse you, but you'll learn to love everything I do to you," Atellus said.

Atellus turned Marcius onto his stomach and entered him. Atellus thrust into Marcius vigorously. It hurt, and Marcius moaned which added to Atellus's enjoyment.

Later, Atellus sent Marcius to his bedroom to wait for him. He told him to be kneeling naked in front of the footstool when he got there. Atellus did not hurry to his bedroom. He wanted Marcius to be really frightened by the time he got there. Atellus went to his bedroom to find that Marcius had obeyed him. Marcius was shivering with fear and cold. Atellus walked to the cupboard and opened it.

"Please master," Marcius begged. "Please don't use the rod on me. Punish me some other way. Please master."

Atellus looked down at Marcius's terrified face, then he reached down and gently stroked his face.

"Do you deserve the rod, slave?" Atellus asked.

"I deserve what you decide, master," Marcius said.

Atellus reached into the cupboard, but he took out a strap instead of the birch rod. He picked Marcius up off his knees and took him over to the bed. Marcius knew that Atellus was going to hurt him, but he also instinctively knew that a strap would hurt less than the birch rod. Atellus sat on the bed, placed the naked youth over his lap, and gave him twenty or so hard, slow evenly distributed smacks across his buttocks and the backs of his thighs. When he had finished, he ordered Marcius to stand up, which Marcius did shakily.

"Thank me, bitch," Atellus said.

"Thank you, master," Marcius said wearily.

"Get on your knees in front of me and kiss my feet. I expect to see some real gratitude," Atellus said.

Marcius fell to his knees in front of his owner and bent over to kiss his feet. Marcius was still crying, and Atellus liked the feel of his slave boy's tears on his feet. But he reached down, grabbed Marcius by his long hair and forced him to look up at him.

"Stop sniveling, you cowardly little brat, or I'll give you something to cry about. Perhaps I should birch you soundly every day; that would toughen you up," Atellus said.

"No, master. Please don't," Marcius sobbed.

Atellus was now fully erect, and he lifted his bottom up from the bed slightly, so he could pull up his tunic.

"Get on with it, slave," he said.

Marcius took his owner's penis into his mouth and started to suck. Once he tasted some salty drops on his tongue he quickened his movements hoping that his master would be satisfied with climaxing in his mouth. Porcus Atellus grinned and said, "Stop. That's enough. Do you think you're going to get out of it that easily? I know you hate me using your tiny hole, but that's what I keep you for. Get on to the bed."

Marcius scrambled onto the bed and spread his legs as wide as he could. Atellus positioned himself quickly and thrust forcefully into Marcius who could not help screaming.

"Scream all you like, little pig," Atellus muttered.

Marcius spent the whole night in his master's bed and Atellus used him in every way and in every position he could think of. Marcius was amazed that Atellus did not become exhausted and how little sleep he seemed to need. In the morning Atellus told him, "You're an incompetent little whore, but I'll teach you."

Over the next few days, Marcius learned to grovel to Atellus's satisfaction. He seemed to always be on his knees in front of Atellus, kissing his feet, begging for mercy and offering himself by timidly reaching up to caress and arouse Atellus. Sometimes it worked. Atellus had a high sex drive and his exquisite slave's pleading often aroused him. And even if he did punish him later, the punishment would be less severe.

Marcius spent most nights in his master's bed, which was warmer than being in the cellar but a dangerous place to be. But the cellar had its dangers, too. One night, quite late, Atellus and two of his friends came down to the cellar to look for a particular wine Atellus wanted his friends to taste. The three men had been drinking for hours. Marcius had been asleep when the three raucous, drunken men came down the stairs with lamps in their hands. They went to Atellus's wine collection to search. Marcius must have made a sound as one of them turned around.

"I think you have rats down here, Atellus," said Atellus's friend Vibius Menenius Pavo.

"That's just my new bitch. I keep him here when I can't be bothered with him," Atellus explained.

"Why haven't you shown him to us?" Pavo asked. "Everyone is saying that you've bought the prettiest slave boy that's been seen in Rome for years."

That remark appealed to Atellus's vanity as a collector.

"He'll start complaining that you never take him anywhere," Pavo added.

"He won't dare complain about anything," Atellus said. "Come look at him if you like."

Atellus lead his friends over to the corner where Marcius was chained. The men placed their lamps in various positions on the floor, so some light would be shed on Marcius. Marcius saw how drunk they were and cringed away from them in fear. He knew what Atellus was like when he was drunk.

"I see," said Pavo. "Are you sure it's not a girl? It's prettier than most girls. He's very blond. Is that natural?"

Atellus looked at Marcius for a few moments.

"See for yourself if you like," Atellus said to Pavo.

To his other friend he said, "Go tell the others they can come down here and use my bitch if they're in the mood."

As the other friend went up the stairs, Pavo knelt on the floor near Marcius and started to pull his blankets off him. He got hold of Marcius and with amazing dexterity in the situation removed his loincloth. Marcius struggled and looked at his owner. Marcius started to beg for mercy. He had been raped before but never by a group of men, and he had no idea how many of his master's friends were upstairs.

"Please don't do this to me, master. I can't do it. Please don't make me. They'll tear me, injure me."

Atellus frowned. Even in the semi darkness he found Calcus's cane.

"Hold him down for me," he said to Pavo. "I'll warm him up for us."

By the time six of Atellus's friends were coming down the stairs, Atellus was beating Marcius with the cane.

"Take it easy, Julius," Pavo said. "He's the kind who faints. It's not the same when they faint."

Marcius tried not to cry, not to whimper in front of the men, but he was frightened, and Atellus was hurting him. He struck Marcius across his buttocks about a dozen times.

"Sniveling bitch," Atellus sneered. "You can have him first if you want, Vibius."

"Thanks," said Pavo. Pavo went to Marcius and knelt behind him. Marcius offered no resistance as Pavo pulled his legs wide apart and knelt between them. He pushed himself into the weeping youth. Pavo had some difficulty entering Marcius.

Although Pavo was drunk, he thought he can't be that new to this. Julius would not do this to a slave who isn't used to it.

Each man took his turn. Marcius wished he could faint. He knew that would not stop them, but at least he would not feel the pain and humiliation of what the men were doing to him.

Maybe he'll kill me. He can't hurt me and frighten me any more once I'm dead, Marcius thought.

The men laughed as they went up the stairs back to the main part of the house. But Atellus remained in the cellar and found the cane again.

"I'm not finished with you yet, bitch," he said to Marcius. "I have to punish you for being such a slut."

Pavo stopped half way up the stairs and turned to look at Atellus and Marcius. As Pavo watched, he expected Marcius to try to get away from Atellus. Instead, the slave crawled closer to his master, kissed his feet and whispered, "Please no more, master. You'll kill me if you beat me again. Please don't kill me. Whip me tomorrow, master. Please! Whip me tomorrow!"

Pavo had seen Atellus mistreat many slaves, but he had never heard such fear in a slave's voice before. He walked down the stairs and put his hand on Atellus's arm as he was about to raise the cane. Pavo knew it was pointless to appeal to him to have some compassion as he knew that his friend had no compassion, so he appealed to his greed instead.

"Your bitch is right, Atellus. You'll kill him. You can punish him properly with a whipping tomorrow. You paid so much for him. You are going to sell him when you're finished, aren't you?" Pavo asked.

Atellus absorbed what Pavo was telling him and dropped the cane on the floor.

"Tomorrow bitch," he snarled at Marcius then turned and started up the stairs. As Pavo watched, Marcius crawled painfully back to the straw in the corner. But that seemed to exhaust him. As Marcius ineffectually reached out for his blankets, Pavo went over to him. Marcius looked at him in terror. Pavo did not think that he had ever seen someone so afraid.

"It's all right, slave," Pavo said as he placed and neatened the blankets over Marcius's prone body. He realized that the slave would need the blankets overnight in the cellar. Marcius was still looking at him fearfully, but he managed to say "Thank you, sir."

"Shit," said Pavo. "You don't have to thank me for something like that."

Pavo also thought how old is he? This one looks younger than Julius's other boys.

CHAPTER 5

The promised whipping had to be postponed. Calcus had decided to check on Marcius at dawn and found him white as a sheet, unconscious under his blankets. He ran up the stairs to tell Atellus who ordered him to send one of the kitchen slaves for his doctor. Calcus and Lucretius carried Marcius upstairs to a small storeroom near the kitchen, which was usually used as a sickroom for ill slaves. All the other household slaves were stunned and frightened. They all knew Atellus's cruelty, but as far as they knew, he had never actually killed anyone.

I would have been more careful, Atellus told himself, if I had not been so drunk.

As it was, his memory of the evening's events was somewhat sketchy.

I didn't mean to kill him, he thought. I want to make him perfect: the most beautiful, most appealing but most obedient slave in Rome.

Atellus's doctor, who had treated him for years and many of his victims asked Atellus, "Do you want the short version or the long version?"

"Since you're my doctor not my mother, the short version will do," said Atellus.

"Your slave is not healthy enough to play your games, Atellus. He is simply not physically strong enough. He probably had never been that strong. If you don't want to kill him, you'll have to punish him less and give him better living conditions," the doctor said.

"He needs some discipline," Atellus said.

"He's hardly more than a child. I find it hard to believe he is so difficult, so rebellious that he needs to be regularly thrashed. There must be other ways of keeping him in order," the doctor said.

Atellus nodded.

A few days later, Atellus discussed Marcius with Calcus.

"You don't want him sent back to the cellar?" Calcus asked.

"No. He'll get ill again if we chain him up. The sick room can be locked, can't it? Atellus asked

"Yes master," Calcus said.

"And it's close to your room?" Atellus asked.

"Almost next door," Calcus said.

"Leave him there then. You can lock him in and keep an eye on him for me," Atellus said.

"And if any of the other slaves become ill?" Calcus asked.

"Move him to a storeroom. There's no shortage of storerooms in the slaves' quarters," Atellus said.

"He could go to the dormitory with the other lads," Calcus suggested.

"No, the stronger lads would take advantage of him. Especially that randy Persian. Speaking of which, send him to me, Calcus, once you get back to the slave quarters."

"Yes master," said Calcus.

But before he left the room he said, "About Marcius?"

"Yes,"

"Can I have him now?" Calcus asked.

"Yes, but be very careful. Don't give him more than ten strokes of the cane. And make sure I haven't punished him too recently," Atellus said.

Although Calcus was pleased with Atellus plans for Marcius, he rather resented the tone of Atellus last remarks.

I know what I'm doing, Calcus thought. I did not make him ill. I don't get so drunk that I don't know what I'm doing.

For the next two days Marcius drifted in and out of consciousness. During that time Cleon nursed him. He sponged him and dressed him in a clean tunic. He applied a soothing, antiseptic ointment left by the doctor to his injuries. He helped him when he needed to use a bucket. He even managed to feed him water and some broth. After a few days, when Marcius was feeling stronger and could do these things for himself, Marcius was embarrassed about the intimate care Cleon had taken of him. Cleon did not at first understand why Marcius blushed when he came near him one morning.

"What's the matter, Marcius?" he asked.

"Did you wash me when I was ill?" he asked.

"Yes," Cleon said. "You were a real mess after what those bastards did to you. Are you embarrassed?"

Marcius nodded.

"Oh Marcius," said Cleon and grinned.

"What?"

"Who else was going to do it? And besides ..."

"Besides ... what?"

"You're acting as if no man has ever touched you before, and we both know that's not true."

"You haven't," said Marcius.

Cleon stopped smiling and looked at Marcius.

"Not because I haven't wanted to," Cleon said. "Do you want me to touch you?"

"I think so," said Marcius. "It would be nice to be with someone gentle again like ..."

"Like who?" Cleon asked.

"Like Gordius."

"Gordius? That big brute!"

"He wasn't a brute!" Marcius said and his face flushed.

"Sorry," said Cleon "I just assumed from the look of him."

"Well, you shouldn't have. He was always gentle."

"You're right, Marcius. I should know better. Some of those big, rough looking men are very gentle. But we can't do anything without their permission. At first I wasn't supposed to even talk to you although Calcus has changed his mind about that. But if we did anything and they caught us, Calcus and Atellus would beat the shit out of both of us."

Life for Marcius became better in some ways once he was well. He was no longer chained in the cellar and, although he was usually locked in his room at night, he was allowed to move around the house and in the garden during the day. He was even given some work to do in the kitchen alongside Cleon and the Persian slave called Darius. The worse thing was that Calcus kept a close watch on him, and, if not permitted to punish Marcius as severely as he would have liked, he could still cane him for the slightest offense, especially in front of the other slaves. Most evenings, if Atellus had sent for one of the other youths instead of Marcius, Calcus would go to Marcius's room. The first time he took his cane with him. Cleon had warned Marcius that this was likely to happen.

“Just do everything he tells you,” Cleon advised. “He’s not as bad as Master Atellus.”

“What do you mean he’s not as bad? They’re exactly the same,” Marcius asked.

“No they’re not. I know that they both like to hurt, but you can follow how Calcus’s mind works. You can bargain with him, or I can, at any rate, and you can learn to,” said Cleon.

“You can bargain with Master Atellus too – sometimes,” Marcius commented.

“Yes, but you never know really where you are,” Cleon said.

“Well,” said Marcius. “He is a madman.”

Marcius was lucky that Calcus did not know of that comment when he spent his first evening with Marcius. He was harsh enough with him as it was. He had waited longer than he had expected and decided to thoroughly enjoy himself. He slapped Marcius and he caned him, but he particularly enjoyed forcing him to please him in all the ways Atellus made him please him. Calcus liked the way Marcius when he begged for mercy called him master instead of sir for the first time.

Afterwards, after he had returned to his bed with Cleon sleeping beside him, Calcus thought I don’t know what the master means when he says Marcius isn’t good in bed. He might not be as experienced as Cleon, but then who the hell is?

After a few weeks, Calcus thought that Atellus was tiring of Marcius. Although Atellus still sent for Marcius regularly, he spent an equal amount of time with Cleon and Darius. So he was not really surprised when one afternoon Atellus gave Calcus a tunic for Marcius to wear and instructions to prepare him for a guest. Calcus watched as Marcius bathed himself. Then he handed him a jar of depilatory cream and told him to use it.

“I used it on my face yesterday, sir,” Marcius said.

Marcius was so fair that he really did not need to use the cream on his face more than once every three days or so, rather to the annoyance of some of the darker skinned youths in the household such as Cleon.

Calcus grinned.

"Your body hair not your face," he explained.

"All of it?" Marcius asked.

Calcus, who was not without a sense of humor, kept smiling.

"It's not like there's much of it," he commented.

So Calcus watched as Marcius carefully smoothed the cream over his chin, legs, chest, belly and on his pubic hair. He sat down beside the bath and waited for the cream to have its effect before climbing into the bath and rinsing himself off. Luckily for Marcius, although the cream had an odd, unpleasant smell, it did not irritate his skin. Calcus thought all this somewhat unnecessary in his view as Marcius had such fine, blond sparse body hair. Once Marcius was denuded of body hair, of course, he did look even younger. The tunic that Marcius put on was made from light blue silk and embroidered with silver thread. It was obviously worth a great deal of money. Calcus noticed how blue Marcius's eyes looked once he was dressed. The effect was, in short, breathtaking. Although, as Calcus escorted Marcius back to his room, he thought uneasily I hope the master doesn't start fancying really young boys.

Atellus's guest was a stout man in his late forties, but he smiled at Marcius in a friendly way when he came into Atellus's dining room. The men were finishing their dinner.

"By all the gods, Atellus. I haven't seen such a pretty slave boy in years. Where did you find such a delightful little Ganymede?" Atellus's guest asked.

The guest gestured to invite Marcius to share his couch at the dining table. Uncertain what to do, Marcius looked at his master. Atellus smiled coldly and nodded. Although the guest continued to chat to Atellus, he could not keep his hands off Marcius. He stroked and caressed him. Soon, Marcius was ordered to show the man to the best guest room in the mansion.

This man, Decius Horatius Bassus was in no hurry to enjoy the beautiful youth. Marcius sat on the bed while the man poured two cups of wine and brought one over to him.

"Don't be nervous, little Gaul," he said.

After the wine, he undressed the youth and then himself.

What a beautiful young man, Bassus thought. And so young and sweet looking. It's a pity about the bruises and stripes.

Bassus knew how much Atellus enjoyed punishing his slaves, and he expected to see marks and bruises on his pets, but it seemed a shame, to him, to mark such a beautiful young man. To him, this slave seemed a gentle and obedient lad.

Marcius knew it did not matter what he thought of his master's friend. He had to please this friend of his master, or he would be punished. And Bassus's pleasant face and manner reassured Marcius.

Besides, he doesn't seem to want to hurt me, Marcius thought.

Bassus did not want to hurt Marcius. He enjoyed kissing and touching Marcius before putting him on his knees in front of him. Marcius did his best to please. When Bassus placed Marcius on his stomach on the bed, he gently and lavishly applied lubricant to him before entering him. As Bassus was smaller than Atellus or Calcus, he did not hurt Marcius. In the morning, he used the sleepy slave again. He cuddled him afterwards. Marcius thought of Gordius and thought how much he missed being cuddled and treated affectionately by someone.

Marcius expected to be dismissed and sent back to the kitchen. Instead the man took his hand and took him to Atellus's private bathroom. Atellus was already in his bath with Cleon and Darius. Atellus seemed to be in one of his rare good moods. He was quite pleased with himself that morning. He had spent an interesting night conquering Greece and Persia as he thought of it and was reasonably content with his slaves.

"I hope Marcius was satisfactory," he said to his friend as the older man got into the bath.

"More than that," his friend commented. "He's as delightful as all your other boys, Atellus."

As Bassus left after breakfast with his host he thought, I wonder if he enjoys sweets the way Cleon does.

But back in his room, Marcius was quiet and thoughtful.

"That old boy was alright to you, wasn't he?" Cleon asked.

"Yes, fine," Marcius said.

Suddenly, Calcus appeared in the doorway. It was frightening how quietly Calcus could move around the house and pounce. He had obviously heard the youths' conversation. He stepped forward and gave Cleon a smack to his behind, but it was a very light slap. In fact, Cleon grinned.

"Do not refer to the master's friend as an old boy," Calcus said, but he did not sound really angry. Cleon then did something that amazed Marcius. He turned to face Calcus, looked up into his face, and smiled that knowing, sensuous smile of his. Then he said, "I'm sorry, master. I didn't mean to be disrespectful. I'll make up for it later."

As Cleon said this he reached out and gently and intimately touched Calcus. Calcus could not stop himself grinning back.

"Yes you will, little whore. Now, both of you get to the kitchen and ask Lucretius for some work to do."

On the way to the kitchen, Marcius whispered to Cleon, "What did you do that for?"

Cleon shrugged. "He likes it, and it got me out of trouble, didn't it?"

That afternoon, Marcius was allowed to have a rest in his room. He heard noises coming from Calcus's room and recognized Cleon's voice. It sounded like Cleon was being punished but it did not sound very serious. Marcius heard him say ouch, but he also heard him say quite distinctly, "Oh come on, master. Not so hard. You want me to enjoy it, too, don't you?"

Marcius heard Calcus laugh.

I'm never going to know as much as Cleon, Marcius decided.

Now that he was giving him to his friends, Atellus's interest in Marcius seemed to return. He sent for him at least once a day. Calcus was pleased with this turn of events, as it meant that Cleon was available to him more often. Marcius never went near his master without a sense of dread, but, although Atellus threatened him with a birching often enough, he usually punished him by strapping him across the back or putting him over his knees for a spanking with a hair brush. Atellus found he liked the way the slightly built youth squirmed across his lap as he wept and begged for mercy. In fact, Marcius always aroused him when he moved like that.

"I'm teaching you to be a whore," Atellus commented. "You'll be a cheap one when you're older."

Every second or so night, Marcius was summoned to the dining room to be introduced to one of his master's important friends. From their conversations, Marcius knew that these men were rich and powerful; there were generals, politicians and businessmen. One rich freedman gave him two silver coins one morning.

"That's just for you for being such a sweet boy."

After his night with Bassus, Marcius became something of a feature at his master's dinner parties. Atellus never seemed to dine alone. Practically every afternoon, guests would arrive for a small dinner party. Most afternoons, at least, Atellus's young drinking companions would arrive. In fact, Pavo seemed to spend so much time there that Marcius wondered why he did not simply move into Atellus's mansion, and save himself a walk every day. Marcius did not know, until Cleon told him, that Pavo came from a family as ancient and aristocratic as Atellus's family, but he was poor. Menenius Pavo was the youngest son of a father who had managed to spend and gamble his way through a once healthy fortune before his early death. He had left no debts, but practically nothing to his numerous children. Pavo received a small allowance from a maternal uncle, which covered his rent and basics like simple foodstuffs, but, for anything else, he was dependent on his best friend Atellus. Whatever his faults, and he had many, Atellus was not stingy. He regarded Pavo's poverty as not due to any fault of his, and he did not treat him with the contempt he treated most people.

The first time Marcius helped Cleon serve at one of his master's small dinner parties, Marcius was terrified that he would spill, drop, or break something. He knew Calcus would cane him later if he did so. But, Marcius was naturally well coordinated, even graceful, and Cleon guided him in his duties and covered for any errors he made. Marcius anxiety was not helped by the fact that the first time he served at table, the guests were his masters' friends who had raped him in the cellar. For this party, Atellus had ordered that Cleon and Marcius be dressed in identical red linen tunics embroidered with golden thread. Calcus knew that red would suit Marcius's fair complexion, but was unsure about Cleon. Cleon also made up his face as well as Marcius's face.

Calcus was quite wrong. Although Cleon was darker than Marcius, both youths looked beautiful.

They look like whores, Calcus thought, but expensive ones. The master's never wrong about this sort of thing.

In fact, as the two slaves entered the dining room, even Atellus's somewhat jaded and cynical friends made appreciative comments.

Once the guests had eaten, drunk, and chatted for a while, and the slaves had cleared away the debris the men settled down for some serious drinking. Cleon and Marcius stood respectfully near the door with their heads slightly bowed. Atellus called Cleon to him. Cleon quickly went to Atellus and lay beside him on his couch with his back to him. As he continued to chat to his friends, Atellus reached out and pulled Cleon's buttocks closer to him. He lifted up Cleon's tunic to reveal Cleon's buttocks, slim hips and thighs and shaved pubic region. Cleon was twenty years of age, and knew his master expected him to become aroused under his touch.

"Hot little Greek bitch, isn't he?" Pavo said to Atellus.

"Do you want the other one?" Atellus asked. "I know you like blonds."

"If you don't mind," Pavo said.

This was not strictly speaking true. Pavo was not very fussy, sexually speaking; he liked any young man or woman who did not expect to be paid. But he had to admit, he was attracted to fair people.

"Come here, slave," Atellus said to Marcius.

Marcius went to Pavo's couch and lay beside him in a similar position to the position Cleon had assumed. He and Pavo had briefly looked each other in the face, and, for a second, Marcius thought he saw some pity for him in Pavo's expression. But, by the time he was lying on his side, and Pavo had started touching him, he decided that he must have imagined the pitying look.

They're not capable of pity, Marcius thought.

Calcus entered the dining room with four more slaves from the dormitory. Atellus's guests pointed to which youth they wished to share their couch. If Cleon and Marcius were the prizes of his slave collection, these youths were all very handsome, healthy slaves. The youths joined their master's guests on their couches and started to please them in the ways they told them to. By this time, Atellus had parted Cleon's buttocks and was thrusting forcefully inside him. Marcius gritted his teeth, expecting Pavo to do the same to him, but Pavo leaned over and whispered very quietly in his ear, "I won't make you. You can suck me if you prefer that."

Marcius nodded and changed position quickly, so he could take Pavo' penis in his mouth. It was humiliating for Marcius to do this in front of everyone, but at least, it did not hurt. Pavo even stroked Marcius's long, fair hair gently as Marcius pleased him with his tongue and mouth. Marcius brought Pavo to climax and swallowed as Atellus always made him do. Atellus had finished with Cleon, and was lying back on his side watching his friend and Marcius. He decided to tease Pavo.

"Why didn't you fuck his bottom? It's what he's for," he said.

"I couldn't resist that little rosebud of a mouth. It looks so pink and pretty tonight. I can fuck him some other time, with your permission, of course," Pavo said.

"Anytime you like," Atellus said casually. "Keep him tonight if you're staying here. You are staying here, aren't you?"

"Yes, I had planned to," Pavo said.

Atellus looked at Marcius.

"I expect my friend to be very pleased with you by tomorrow morning, slave. Or you know what I'll do to you," Atellus said.

"Yes, master," Marcius said timidly.

Marcius accompanied Pavo to a guest room and watched him undress. Pavo yawned, stretched and climbed into bed as Marcius watched him. Pavo looked at Marcius who was still dressed.

"Why aren't you in bed?" Pavo asked.

"You haven't told me what to do, master," Marcius said meekly.

"Do you have to be told everything?" Pavo asked.

"That's what I've been taught, master," Marcius said.

Marcius should not really have been calling Pavo master, as he was not his owner. But Cleon tended to call all his master's friends master, so Marcius chose to do the same.

"He's really broken your will, hasn't he?" Pavo commented.

Marcius did not know what to say. Pavo, like all members of his class, had been brought up to believe that slaves, especially from places like Gaul and Germania, were savage brutes whose wills had to be broken. Pavo believed that if slaves did not live in constant fear of punishment and execution, they would revolt and slaughter their owners. Or at least, flee and the economy would collapse. But, Pavo did not enjoy cruelty for its own sake as his friend did.

"Come to bed, Marcius. All I'm going to do for a few hours is sleep. And, in the morning, I'll tell your master how good, docile, obedient and submissive you were, and how much I enjoyed you. Now, will you get into bed?"

"Yes master. Thank you, master," Marcius said.

In the morning, Pavo woke to find Marcius still sleeping but on the far side of the bed.

If he moves any further away from me, he thought, he'll fall out of bed, but he could understand Marcius's fear.

"Marcius," he said gently. "Come closer to me. I'm not him. I'm not going to hurt you."

Sleepily, Marcius moved closer to Pavo, and Pavo took him into his arms, then caressed and cuddled him as if he was a frightened child or animal. Timidly, Marcius responded to this.

Why is Atellus so cruel to this one? Pavo wondered. He's lovely looking and willing. He really tries to be obedient and pleasing. And it's genuine. You can never tell with Cleon, but this one is like a child compared to Cleon.

Marcius was surprised at the gentle way Pavo touched him. His owner was never gentle. He grabbed him, manhandled him into position, slapped him, held his down and forced him to please him.

"Is he just like that with me?" Marcius had once asked Cleon.

"No, that's how he likes it. He does that to everyone he owns," Cleon said, but Cleon had noticed that Marcius seemed to get more beatings than he did, and for no reason he could understand.

Pavo then did something that really surprised Marcius. He changed position in the bed, so he could take Marcius's semi erect penis in his mouth. Marcius altered his position, so he could do this for Pavo, but he was amazed. Both young men enjoyed sucking while being sucked.

He's a patrician, Marcius thought. A Roman, my owner's friend. Why is doing this for me?

In fact the last person who had sucked Marcius had been Gordius, and he had said, "Don't tell anyone about this, or people will think I'm a girlie like you."

"I don't think anyone would ever say that about you, master," Marcius had replied.

Gordius had laughed and said, "Your cock's a nice mouthful. Why shouldn't I suck it if I feel like it? You do it often enough for me."

Pavo continued to suck Marcius, but Marcius did not expect him to bring him to climax. He was grateful that he was letting him have some pleasure as it was. Pavo stopped and told Marcius to roll onto his stomach. He positioned himself behind him once Marcius submissively spread his legs.

"Where's the ointment?" he asked.

"Master doesn't let me use ointment," Marcius said.

That surprised Pavo. With someone like Cleon, maybe it would not matter, he thought, but this lad hasn't Cleon's experience. He had seen his friend fully erect and knew he was larger than most men. He must really hurt this slave, he thought, especially without any lubricant.

Pavo hesitated but Marcius was aroused and said, "Please, master. I want you to. Please. It will be all right."

Pavo moistened the tips of his fingers and used them to moisten Marcius anus. He then spat on his hand and moistened himself some more. He entered Marcius as carefully as he could and began to move slowly. Marcius had to stifle a cry in the blankets, but he nodded his consent. Pavo moved faster.

"Play with yourself if you want to, if it helps," he said to Marcius.

Marcius would never do such a thing with Atellus, knowing that he would be thrashed for it later. Both men came almost at the same time.

Sweating, Pavo rested briefly on Marcius, before withdrawing and flopping onto his side of the bed.

“Thank you, master,” Marcius said.

“What for?” Pavo asked.

“For being kind, master,” Marcius said.

That’s kindness to him, Pavo thought. Just because I did not deliberately hurt him; he thinks that’s kindness.

CHAPTER 6

Pavo accompanied Atellus part of the way to the Senate the next morning as Atellus was a senator, although, he realized, with some alarm, how increasingly pointless being a senator was now that Julius Caesar was in power. Lucretius took the opportunity to send Marcius with some flowers to the dining rooms, study, and his master's bedroom. Atellus did not want his house filled with flowers, but he appreciated flowers from his gardens as he liked all beautiful things and some flowers in these rooms, so he could put on display some of his finer Egyptian and Greek vases and bowls. Marcius paused briefly to sniff the flowers' scent and touch their delicate petals. Not for the first time, he wondered how his master could have such perfect taste in some things, and yet be so cruel and brutal. When he turned, he saw Calcus looking at him thoughtful.

"Yes, Master Calcus?" he asked respectfully and hoped he was not in trouble for anything. Calcus said mildly, "Hurry up with that, and get back to the kitchen," he said.

"Yes, Master Calcus," Marcius said.

As he left, Calcus wondered which of Atellus's possessions in the room at that moment most people would think more lovely: the flowers, the vase, or the blond, barbarian youth.

Like Pavo before him, he wondered why Atellus seemed to hate Marcius.

Once Atellus returned from a stormy meeting at the Senate, Calcus followed him into his bedroom with the intention of helping him remove his cumbersome toga. But Atellus stopped him, and decided that he was in the mood for some casual cruelty so he told him to send Marcius to him.

"It's about time he learned some basics like helping his master with his toga," he commented to Calcus.

Calcus found Marcius in the kitchen and sent him to Atellus's bedroom. Marcius went wearily. He went into the bedroom, went to his master, and knelt at his feet as he had been taught to do. Marcius had learned to stop what he was doing and stand still when Calcus entered a room when he was working, and wait for further orders, but when his master sent for him or came into a room he had to kneel and bow his head. Atellus decided that Marcius had been too slow obeying his order.

"Too slow, slave. I expect you to hurry here when I send for you. I suppose you were day dreaming about some smelly cave back home in Gaul. A switching will wake you up," Atellus said.

Marcius expected to be ordered to fetch a switch from his master's cupboard, but Atellus instead went to the doorway and shouted "Slave!"

Marcius heard someone scurrying to the bedroom.

"Fetch Calcus," Atellus said to one of his other slaves. "I have a job for him."

Marcius sometimes wondered why his master did not use a bell or something to summon his slaves. He must enjoy shouting like that, he thought, although it must be hard on his throat some days. Marcius kept his eyes downcast as Atellus went to his cupboard and made his selection from his implements of punishment. He was in no hurry as he liked to drag out a slave's punishment. He selected a favorite of his; a medium weight switch. He liked the sound it made when it contacted bare young flesh like Marcius's or Cleon's. Atellus loomed over Marcius and toyed with the switch until Calcus arrived. Atellus enjoyed the preliminary rituals before administering a beating. He liked to upbraid his boy, tell him what his punishment would be, and order him to strip naked and kiss his feet in submission before striking even the first blow. He liked Marcius, in particular, to be frightened and tearful even before the first blow.

Marcius kissed Atellus's feet, but he thought, I'm not going to cry or plead before he hits me. I'm not a child. I was not born a slave like Cleon was. My mother was a queen who chose to die with her people. I am descended from generations of warriors. I'll beg for mercy if I have to, but not before he hits me.

Atellus seemed to sense what Marcius was thinking, so he reached down and pulled his tunic off him. Then he put his hands on the youth's shoulders to hold him still.

"Look at me, bitch. I want to watch you sniveling while you're punished," he said.

Marcius looked up into Atellus's ugly face.

"How many strokes, master?" Calcus asked.

"Ten to start, and lay them on hard. But, take your time about it. I want him to feel every stroke."

Marcius managed not to cry out after the first three hard cuts across his back, but yelped at the fourth. Then he started to cry.

"Nothing to say, slave?" Atellus sneered.

(Thwack!)

"Please, master," Marcius whimpered.

(Thwack!)

"Please, have mercy."

(Thwack!)

"Have some pity."

(Thwack)

"I'm sorry, master. I'm sorry, please no more," Marcius whimpered.

Calcus hit him four or more times across the back, but Marcius was crying too much to speak. Then he said quickly and desperately, "Master. Please no more. Please. I'm sorry. Please, no more master."

Somewhat to his surprise, Atellus nodded to Calcus to indicate that he should stop beating Marcius.

Marcius, hurt and humiliated, hung his head, and his tears fell on his master's feet.

"Kiss my feet, thank me, and promise to be a good boy from now on," Atellus said.

Marcius said between sobs, "Thank you, master. I'll be a good slave. I'll do anything you say. Please, no more master," Marcius said.

Marcius kissed his master's feet as he wept.

Atellus dismissed Calcus and thanked him for his work, but he took the switch from him. Marcius realized that his punishment was not yet over. Atellus went to his bed and put the switch on the bed. He was still wearing his toga, so he ordered Marcius to stand up, come over to him and help him with his toga. As Marcius was sore and shaking, he was clumsy removing the toga.

"Useless," muttered Atellus. "So pretty, but so useless."

Atellus seated himself comfortably at the foot of his bed, and took hold of the switch again.

He grabbed Marcius, and hauled him over his lap. He pulled down his loincloth and removed it.

"Lie still, pretty boy. You're still young enough to benefit from an over the knee beating," Atellus said.

As Atellus beat Marcius young bare bottom, he became fully erect as usual. He liked the way Marcius moved as he beat him. Marcius was soon aware of his owner's excitement. In such close contact and in such a position, he would have been remarkably unaware not to notice his owner's erection. Atellus was no hypocrite. He knew when he put Marcius over his lap to beat him he was doing it for his own erotic pleasure. The suggestion that anyone would do such a thing for any other reason would have made him laugh aloud. Once he was ready, Atellus let Marcius up from across his lap but then pushed him back onto his knees and bent him over the end of the bed. Meekly, Marcius spread his legs and offered his buttocks to Atellus. Atellus thrust roughly into Marcius who screamed in pain. Atellus moved quickly and climaxed quickly. Atellus sat on his bed and watched Marcius whimper on the floor. After a few minutes, he picked him up, dragged him to the doorway and pushed him out of his room.

"Get back to your room, and stay there until Calcus tells you otherwise," Atellus snarled at Marcius. But Cleon had been listening and was nearby, so he helped support Marcius safely back to his tiny room in the slaves' quarters. Cleon tried to calm and comfort Marcius, but there was not really much he could do.

A few weeks later, Atellus decided to educate Marcius further. He took him to a small room attached to his bedroom where he stored his clothes. All of Atellus's clothes were tasteful, conservative and expensive. But in one small chest there were some flashy, showy garments, but they were women's garments. There were even some wigs.

He likes to dress up? Marcius wondered, then he worked it out.

That's next. He wants me to dress up, Marcius thought.

Atellus looked at the dresses.

"Which one do you like?" he asked Marcius mockingly.

"The pink one. That's pretty," Marcius said.

"You have no taste," Atellus commented.

Marcius shrugged.

"I'm a barbarian and a slave. Why should I have any taste, master?" Marcius asked.

"No, you shouldn't," Atellus admitted. He gave Marcius the dress, some short of undergarment, and told him to see if any of the pairs of women's sandals fitted him. Then he went into his bedroom while Marcius changed his clothes. Marcius decided that there was something odd about the woman's shift he had been given. Once he put it on he saw that there was padding in the front where a woman's breasts would be. Once he put on the pink dress his figure did look more womanly well, he looked more like a small breasted woman with slim hips. One pair of sandals did just fit him. Atellus called out, "Hurry up, slave."

Marcius felt ridiculous as he entered the bedroom. Atellus had placed his chair in front of the table and told Marcius to sit down. Small pots of lotion and cosmetics had appeared from somewhere and were on the table. Atellus untied Marcius hair, and brushed it for him.

"I'm glad no one's cut your hair. I'm going to make you look like a real girl."

Marcius did have fine, thick blond hair, which was trimmed but not cut short. It was quite long. And he had darker eyelashes and eyebrows, so he did not have that odd look that some very fair people have. Atellus applied make up to Marcius. Once he had finished painting his face, Atellus handed Marcius a mirror, so he could see the result of his handiwork. The result was surprisingly natural and subtle, but Marcius realized that Atellus must have made up many of his slaves over the years.

"You look like my mother," Atellus commented.

"What?" Marcius said without thinking. "She was pretty?"

Atellus's face flushed with anger. He pulled Marcius up from the chair and held him tightly by the upper arms. He stared into Marcius's face.

"What? What did you say? A monster like me couldn't have had a pretty mother! I'll birch you for that later, but in the meantime," Atellus said.

Atellus sat on his chair, hauled Marcius across his lap and applied a wooden hairbrush to his bottom with real force. Marcius cried out, "Please. I didn't say it. I didn't."

Marcius knew that his master was genuinely furious with him and would use both the brush and the birch on him. Atellus beat him with the brush until his arm was tired, then he dumped him on the floor in front of him. Atellus needed some time to get his breath back. Marcius whimpered, "Please, master. I did not mean that."

"What did you mean?"

"I don't know. I wasn't thinking. I did not mean to be insulting."

"It doesn't matter. You going to get a thrashing tonight anyway. But first, I'm having a party a special party with some special friends of mine."

"Your friends will kill me, master," Marcius said. "They almost did last time."

"This will be different. They will be other slaves there. I'm going to show you off. You, Cleon and Darius are going to perform for my guests. Cleon and Darius will show you what to do. Then I'll keep you to myself for the rest of the party. My friends will want you, especially dressed as a girl."

Marcius would have loved to say, "If you ever lose all you money, you could become a pimp," but he knew that making such a comment would be the same as committing suicide.

Atellus then handed Marcius some ointment.

"Apply this to your bottom. You're going to need it. None of your nonsense or crying tonight in front of my guests. Remember that you're already earned a flogging, but that the number of lashes I'm going to give you depends on how you behave tonight."

Atellus escorted Marcius to his small, private dining room which Marcius had never been to before. This was where Atellus held his parties, which people gossiped about. There seemed to be little food on the table, but plenty of wine. As Marcius entered the room he heard Cleon say, "Cut it out, Darius. We haven't started yet."

"Always the professional," Darius sneered.

"Persian bastard," Cleon muttered.

"Greek bitch," said Darius.

Darius and Cleon often talked to each other like this, and were often caned for it by Calcus.

"It's not easy keeping peace between Greece and Persia," joked Atellus to Calcus who just looked at him.

One day, Atellus thought. I'm going to buy myself a better educated butler.

Darius was one of Atellus's current favorites a very handsome, dark, healthy peasant lad. Both Darius and Cleon stared at Marcius when he came into the room. They both had acknowledged long ago how delicately pretty Marcius was, but Cleon decided that he had never seen a boy who could pass for a girl so easily. And Cleon had seen many boys dressed up as girls. Male guests arrived with their own slaves. After a few drinks, all the youths except Marcius were stripped naked and passed around. Atellus sent his three pets to the floor in front of the couches. Not knowing what to do, Marcius let Cleon and Darius kiss him, lift up the woman's dress, touch him, position him and finally take turns using Marcius's mouth and bottom. Cleon whispered into his ear, "Try to relax. Don't think about it. We'll do everything."

Atellus and his guests found this entertainment arousing. Atellus also noticed how gentle Cleon had tried to be with Marcius. Pavo, who lay on the couch beside him, noticed, too, and said, "Your Greek and Gaul are in love. I hope you're not jealous."

Atellus laughed and beckoned to Marcius. Although he gave Darius and Cleon to his guests that evening, he kept Marcius to himself. He used him in front of his friends, but he was not in the mood to share him. Watching the fair slave, however, at least three of the guests decided to borrow Marcius in the future. As one wealthy patrician later commented, "He is unusual. He looks like the love child of a barbarian princess." He had no idea how close he was to guessing the truth about Marcius.

At the end of the evening and after the guests had departed, Atellus picked up an exhausted Marcius from his couch, and half dragged him to his bedroom.

"Do you remember what I promised you, slave?" Atellus demand.

"Yes, master," Marcius said.

"Do I have to tie you down?" he asked.

"No, master. I'll keep still. I'll do my best to keep still," Marcius said wearily.

Atellus beat him for a long time with the rod. It was not as hard, perhaps, as Marcius's first birching, but it was the hardest beating he had had since then. Marcius cried, but he did not try to get away or beg for mercy. He knew that Atellus might beat him to death and he no longer cared. But Atellus liked it when

Marcius pleaded for mercy so he said, "Beg me to stop, bitch," Atellus said.

Marcius caught his breathe, sighed, turned to look at his master and said, "Please son. Mummy's sorry. She loved you all along; she just didn't know how to show it." Marcius smiled cynically at Atellus.

I might be a barbarian, Marcius thought. But I'm clever enough to work out what's wrong with him.

That was too much for Atellus. He picked the youth up and threw him across the room. Marcius fell against a table. He was knocked unconscious, and his head wound started to bleed.

The slaves in the kitchen heard the crash, and Lucretius asked Calcus what they should do.

"We go if we're called," Calcus said.

They were called, and a bleeding Marcius was laid on a kitchen table. Lucretius tied a cloth around Marcius's head, but the injury looked serious to him.

"I'm going for the doctor," Lucretius said.

"The master did not say to ..." Calcus said.

"If you get in my way, you festering worm," said Lucretius. "I will knock you down."

The doctor came quickly and examined the injured slave. The doctor knew that it was sheer luck that Atellus had not killed Marcius.

"He looks so young," he said to Lucretius. "Doesn't he have friends anywhere?"

"I'll try to find out when he recovers. He will live, won't he?"

"For the time being," the doctor commented grimly.

"Can't you do something about the master?" Lucretius asked.

"I'm a freedman," the doctor said. "But I can suggest a new sedative to him. He does suffer from insomnia. A powerful sedative might keep him calmer with this boy."

"Thanks," said Lucretius.

Atellus was in a stupor for days. His doctor told him he was ill, had a fever and needed rest. As he did not even feel much like sex, Atellus assumed he was quite ill. He did not know that his chef and doctor were feeding him a very high dose of a powerful sedative. If they gave him anymore, they were in danger of sending him to sleep forever. They were tempted, but to do so was too risky. If they were caught, every slave in the household would be put to death, including Marcius.

Meanwhile, Lucretius went to the arena and found Antonius. Antonius was due to leave Rome soon and move into his new business; a pleasant, small tavern on the seaside in southern Italy. Antonius still felt guilty about how he had sold Marcius to Atellus, but he said to Lucretius, "What can I do? I've spent almost all the money."

"Think of something. He'll kill that poor boy," Lucretius said.

Antonius asked the arena manager and the kitchen manager for some advice. All they could suggest was raising a loan from someone rich.

"Who do I know who's rich?" Antonius asked.

"Only Madame Flavia," someone joked.

The latest gossip was that Flavia had just added another brothel to her expanding business empire.

"What did you say?" Antonius asked the kitchen manager.

"Just Madame Flavia. Sorry. Stupid joke," the manager said.

"Wait! Flavia. Gordius said that Flavia has met Marcius and made an offer for him at a party," Antonius said.

"Are you serious? I mean. Was she serious?" the kitchen manager asked.

"I don't know. I can't remember what Gordius said happened exactly."

"It's worth going to see her and asking her if she's interested in Marcius. What do you have to lose?" asked the arena manager quietly.

Flavia was busy with her accounts when Antonius went to see her. Flavia did not actually know Antonius, but she remembered that he had been Gordius's friend and manager, and she had always liked Gordius. She saw Antonius immediately as his distress was evident to everyone in her office. As Antonius entered her office, she was shouting at her accountant, Abraham Ben Joseph, "Of course some of my managers cheat me. If anyone cheats me over ten percent, tell me."

"Why? What will you do?" Abraham asked.

"I'll send a couple of my big Africans over to smack some heads together. This is Rome, Abraham. There's a war. There's always a war on somewhere. I own taverns and brothels. While there's a Roman army; I won't go broke."

Flavia quickly grasped Antonius's problem and made one of her quick decisions.

"Yes. I remember that pretty fair boy. I thought this might happen," she said. "I'll buy him from Atellus."

"Just like that?" Antonius asked. "Will Atellus sell?"

"He will to me," Flavia said.

"Why?" Antonius.

"First, I'm going to offer him twice what he paid you for him," she said.

"Can you afford that?" Antonius asked.

"Yes, with a bit of shifting money around. I can call in some debts, borrow from my investors if I have to. Don't sigh like that, Abraham; I know what I'm doing," she said.

"Isn't Atellus rich?" Antonius asked.

"Yes, but he's greedy and he spends a lot. He'd like to be richer," Flavia said. "Besides, Atellus does get bored very quickly with these slave boys. He rarely keeps one more than three months. And ..." she began to say.

"Yes?" Antonius asked.

"I've been in this business for more than twenty years and I know everyone's secrets including Atellus and his family," she said.

"They have a secret?" Antonius asked.

"Doesn't every family?" Flavia asked.

"Are you going to give me a hint?" Antonius asked.

"Let's say that someone like Atellus would not like everyone in Rome to know where his father really met his mother," said Flavia.

"What? The old senator? They were childhood sweethearts, weren't they? From some like town in Northern Italy, weren't they?" Antonius asked.

He realized that Flavia was smiling at him.

"You don't mean," he said.

Flavia nodded.

"Pretty little thing, but a rotten mother. She should not have rejected Atellus like that. She must have known the risk she was taking marrying Atellus's father."

"What about his father?" Antonius asked.

"The old senator? Compared to him, a frog was attractive. He just made jokes about his appearance. But Atellus could never cope. Poor Atellus," she commented.

"Poor Atellus!" Antonius said.

"He can't help it," Flavia said. "He's not sane. Still, I'll see Atellus as soon as I can. I'll call on him. He'll like that."

Once Atellus's household slaves learned that the notorious Madame Flavia was intending to visit Atellus, his health started to improve dramatically. She dressed discreetly for this private visit between friends. Atellus was in bed, but less sleepy when Flavia talked to him.

After a few polite questions about his health, she said, "I want to buy your slave from Gaul, while he's still in one piece. Three thousand denarii, she offered.

"How much?"

"You heard me. Three thousand denarii," Flavia said.

"Aren't we going to haggle?" Atellus asked.

(This was Rome where people haggled over the price of one apple).

"I'm not in the mood today," Falvia said.

Considering the price that Flavia was willing to pay, Atellus decided that he was tired of Marcius anyway.

But later he asked himself, what is it about Marcius? Is he Flavia's long lost son or something?

"But," he said to Flavia. "I don't want him talking about me to everyone who matters in Rome."

"I'll tell him to be discreet. It is something of a professional obligation in his case and mine. It's the same with doctors and lawyers. By the way, I want him now," she said.

"I'm not sure if he's well enough. There was an ... um ... accident," he said.

"I heard he'd had a fall," she said tactfully. "But, I can send my litter with my doctor. He can consult with yours and decide when this Marcius is well enough to travel. We are only talking about moving him a few streets away from here."

"What are you going to do with him?" Atellus asked.

"Put him in my best house," Flavia said.

"You're not taking him into your home?" Atellus asked.

Atellus, like everyone else in Rome, knew that Flavia was a soft touch with a tendency to take in stray animals and lost children whom no one else wanted.

"My home?" she asked. "With my teenage daughters in the house? That bunch of little flirts! I like the look of the lad, but I don't want him fathering my grandchildren. Besides, I'm a businesswoman. Marcius is the prettiest slave I've seen in years, maybe decades, and people will talk about him. I think that I'll get my investment back; I usually do."

CHAPTER 7

A few days later, Flavia's litter departed from her house. Her African litter bearers were an impressive sight. Someone from out of town would assume that a consul's wife was going past. Except, a patrician would never have a litter in such a bright shade of red. All Rome knew Flavia's litter. Flavia did somewhat ruin the impressive effect by running after her litter bearers, shouting last minute instructions, "Take it easy with him, lads. I don't need the litter for hours. Listen to the doctor."

Two of the litter bearers could not help grinning, and Flavia's eldest daughter shouted from the doorway, "Mum! You're still in your bathrobe and slippers!"

"What? Oh yeah," Flavia said and hurried back inside her home.

Flavia's doctor examined Marcius and knew that Atellus's doctor was looking after him properly. But he glanced at Atellus's doctor shrewdly.

"And what are you doing to Atellus?" he asked.

"I'm trying a new potion for his insomnia. It's a compound from my part of the world," Atellus's doctor said.

"I think I know that compound," Flavia's doctor said. "Try not to kill him. It might look bad just at the moment."

"It's perfectly safe. Trust me. I'm a doctor. I know these things."

The two doctors exchanged a knowing smile.

Meanwhile, Flavia was waiting impatiently for Marcius to arrive at her home. She told her daughters that a sick relative was coming to stay.

"What relative?" her eldest daughter, Virginia, asked. "We don't have relatives. She doesn't even know who our fathers are."

"How surprising," Flavia's second eldest daughter said.

Now that they were teenagers, Flavia could not exactly hide her profession from her children, and she had never really tried. As small children they had believed their nurse's story that their mother was a successful actress.

"I think she's bought us a brother," said Flavia's youngest daughter.

Her older sisters looked at the twelve-year-old.

"Mother said 'When he gets here you girls are to treat him as your brother. But not like in Egypt.' What does that mean?" she asked.

"It's hard to tell with our mother. We'll just have to wait and find out what's going on from Auntie Claudia as usual," Virginia said.

Flavia went to see Marcius as soon as he was settled in a comfortable bed in her home.

"What's he done to him?" she asked her doctor.

"It looks worse than it is, although he is battered and bruised."

"Is his body scarred?" she asked.

"No. I don't think it will be. Atellus was probably trying to avoid leaving any permanent scars on this slave. He would have been thinking of how much he could sell him for later," the doctor said. "There are lotions and ointments, which will sooth his skin, and help with any pain."

"Good," said Flavia. "He's suffered enough."

"What are you going to do with him?" the doctor asked.

"First, I'm going make sure he gets well. Then, I'm going to do something really unusual; I'm going to discuss with him what he wants to do in the future."

Marcius woke up a few days later in a strange bed in a strange house. A tall, plump fair mature woman was sitting on the bed, and holding his hand. For a groggy moment, he thought she was his mother, but his mother had never worn make up and her hair had not been such a bright shade of red. He realized that he knew the woman.

"Madame Flavia?" he asked.

"That's right, dear. You remember me," she said.

Marcius almost said that Flavia was the sort of person who would be difficult to forget, but he knew that would sound rude, so he said, "You were at one of my master's parties."

"He's not your master, any more. I have bought you from him," she said.

"Yes, mistress," he said.

Flavia laughed and squeezed his hand.

"Don't start that with me! Call me Auntie Flavia like everyone else does."

"Really?" Marcius asked.

"Yes, really," Flavia said. "Now, little Gaul. What am I going to do with you?"

"Anything you like, mistress," Marcius said through sheer force of habit.

"Stop that," she said. "You don't have to grovel to me. It doesn't do a thing for my libido; such as it is these days."

Marcius looked confused.

"Never mind, son. Never mind. I suppose that you know how I make a living?" she asked.

"Yes, Gordius told me that you own taverns and brothels. He said ..."

"Yes."

"That you treat your slaves well. You let them earn their freedom," Marcius said.

"Yes I do. I find that works better than floggings when it comes to getting the best from my ... shall we say ... staff. Strictly speaking, you might not be able to buy love or loyalty, but you can buy reasonably good approximations. Some of my boys and girls work hard for a few years, save some money and buy their freedom from me. Sometimes, I help people set up some sort of shop or business, if I'm asked to help. Now, before we start talking about your future, I need you to answer a question for me. I promise I'm not being nosy, but I need to know."

"What? " Marcius asked.

"You do actually prefer men to girls, don't you? I know that you haven't exactly been given a choice about it in the past. You've done what you've had to in order to survive. I know what happened. It happened to me years ago. But when I saw you at that party with Gordius, I thought, well, you looked like you cared for him, that you felt safe with him. Or were you just grateful that he was kind to you?" she asked.

"I was grateful and he was kind to me. I did not expect him to be. I was so frightened when he bought me. He was a gladiator, a professional killer," Marcius said.

"He did not have much of a choice either," Flavia commented. ""He was a prisoner of war. He could have been worked to death in a field or a mine, so he took his chances as a gladiator."

Marcius thought about Gordius for a few moments then he said, "I did care for him and it wasn't just gratitude. I liked being with Gordius. He was patient and gentle and ... I … um ..."

"You got used to going to bed with him?" she prompted.

The youth nodded.

"I thought so. I'm glad you cared for him, Marcius. He loved you and you made him happy. So you do like men?"

"Not when they're cruel to me like Atellus was. There were a couple of boys back home in Gaul," he began to say and stopped as he was feeling embarrassed.

"Go on, Marcius. You can tell me," Flavia said.

"We didn't do much, just played around mainly."

Flavia patted his hand and smiled at him in an understanding, motherly way.

"I understand, Marcius. It's the same everywhere," she said. "I think I know what we should do, Marcius. I have a house near here. It's quiet, discreet and private. Usually about six of my best boys live there, and they see my best customers. No one mistreats my boys. I don't make any of my slaves do anything revolting or dangerous. Once you're well again, I want you to work there for a few weeks. And if you find it upsetting or disgusting or anything; I won't make you keep working there. I'll find you a job as a household slave. But, if that happens, it could take you decades to earn your freedom."

She paused as she looked at the beautiful youth in the bed.

"And if that happens," she added. "I've wasted a lot of money, my accountant will cry, and every other madam in Rome will think I've gone completely out of my mind."

A few evenings later, Claudia came to dine with Flavia and her daughters. At the end of the meal, she said, "Run along, darlings. Your mother and I have dull business matters to discuss."

Various girls said, "Goodnight mother" and "Goodnight Auntie Claudia," before leaving the table.

"What business matters?" Flavia asked suspiciously.

"Marcius. You are going to put him to work once he's strong enough."

"I'm thinking about it," Flavia said.

"After what you paid for him!" said Claudia.

"I'm not sure he's suited to our profession."

"Not suited. He's gorgeous," Claudia said.

"I know he suited that way. It's just that he's so vulnerable. He reminds me of a lost kitten or puppy. You and I know that a slave, any slave has to learn to grovel to his owner, but it's become second nature to him."

"Look at who he's belonged to. You and I know that Gordius the Thracian was a decent man, but his appearance was intimidating, and little Marcius must have been terrified of him at first before he got to know him properly. And Porcius Atellus is a madman. He is perhaps the cruelest master in Rome, and as you know, there's a fair amount of competition for that title. That Marcius has survived shows that he's not stupid. Don't tell me you were never an unfortunate slave in need of help and protection."

"I know I was, but later when I acted humble I did it because they expected it. I was acting a role, playing a part. Was I any good?" Flavia asked.

"Not really," Claudia said.

"Why not?"

"You used to get the giggles whenever you tried to act pathetic," Claudia said.

"Oh yes. I remember. But you were brilliant at that. All the big, strong butch Roman soldiers wanted to look after you and stop you crying," Flavia said.

Even if Flavia was the better businesswoman, she knew that Claudia had always been better at manipulating men.

"I can't see Marcius acting a role," Flavia said.

"Because he hasn't been taught to," Claudia said.

"What?"

"Well. We were taught to behave in certain ways once we got to Rome, weren't we? If anyone can turn that pretty slave into a high class whore, it's you Flavia. You can protect him. You can teach him to be pleasant to the customers without getting involved with them. I've seen you do it. You've trained slaves who were less promising than Marcius. You were one of the best paid whores in Rome yourself once," Claudia said.

"I was good in my day," said Flavia. "We both were."

"How old were you when you came to Rome?" Claudia asked.

"Fourteen," Flavia said.

"Did you speak Latin?" Claudia asked.

"No, of course not," said Flavia.

"Neither did I. We learned it when we got here. And Auntie Cordelia paid for us to have lessons in Latin, singing, dancing, music, conversation. She knew we could do more than just have sex with the customers. Men paid for our company as well. Don't you remember all that work we had to do?"

"I remember the switchings I got from the old witch," Flavia said.

"Because you wouldn't pay some attention during lessons. That irritated her. She had high hopes for you. You were her pet."

"I was not!"

"You were, too!"

Twenty years previously, they would have poked their tongues out at each other at this stage of their discussion, but they considered themselves too mature for that now. They were not aware that their conversation had not really changed much since then.

"I never was very good at music," Flavia said.

"But you made them laugh," Claudia said. "They liked talking to you. And if they wanted to talk about their problems, you listened."

"Well," Flavia said. "They were paying for my time. If they just wanted someone to talk to, that was fine with me."

Claudia suddenly asked, "Whatever happened to that dreamy, quiet boy. He was very studious, very shy. His father paid because you always cheered him up."

"He's one of the leaders in the Senate now,' Flavia said.

"Oh yes, so he is. Well, you must have done something for his self confidence," Claudia said.

"He was only a kid then. I knew he'd do well in the long run. What were we talking about before we started down memory lane?"

"Um ... Marcius," Claudia said.

"Yes, Marcius is obviously bright. Who knows what his talents are?" Flavia said.

"He does move well. Most boys his age clump along, but he walks really gracefully, like some dancers do."

“Yes. He does now that you mention it. I hadn’t really noticed but you’re right. And that must come naturally. They don’t dance much in Gaul fight yes, dance no.”

“How do you know so much about Gaul?” Claudia asked.

“How do you think?”

“Oh, yes sorry. I forgot. You’re from Gaul, aren’t you?”

“Originally,” said Flavia. “And you’re from Macedonia. Or was it Thrace?”

“It was Macedonia,” Claudia said.

It was not difficult to find tutors for Marcius. Between them Flavia and Claudia knew most of Rome’s better actors, dancers and musicians. In fact, they had helped many of them at the start of their careers. Marcius’s Latin teacher worked on his conversation skills, improved his knowledge of Roman conventions, and much improved his reading of Latin. But he commented to Flavia, “His Latin is good anyway. He’s had teachers before me. He must have learned it as a child in Gaul.”

“From soldiers?” Flavia suggested.

“I don’t think so. A soldier might chat up a pretty, local boy; but I don’t think he’d bother to teach him to read the language.”

“Perhaps his dad’s a Roman soldier and his mum is a Gaul. It happens all the time. He’s spoken both languages when he was child. I don’t think I care. It means he won’t have to work too hard,” Flavia said.

Marcius’s new music teacher came to see Flavia with a big grin on his face.

“He can play a flute and he has a sweet voice. With training, he could be quite good. He played me some simple tunes from his homeland, simple but pleasant, and I have not heard them before. I asked if those tunes were written down anywhere, but he said he just seemed to remember them from when he was a child. And he did look rather sweet as he played his wooden flute. Very appealing in fact."

"And you can teach him other tunes, from all over, if you think he has some talent," Madam Flavia suggested.

"Oh yes. I think he has some talent, and I think he might like that. When he was playing he had that look on his face that only people who like to play music get, a sort of concentrating look."

Rome's best dancer did not come to Flavia with good news.

"He's graceful, well coordinated and very pretty, but he'll never be a dancer," he said.

"Why not?"

"He's too old to start, and, well, he just did not really seem to understand what I was trying to teach him. He did try because he wants you to be pleased with him," the dancer said.

"Well," Madam Flavia said philosophically, "I buy my slaves for their looks and if one of my boys or girls can also sing, dance, or play a musical instrument, that's just a bonus. It's not exactly what I buy them for."

"He did say that he had been trained as a cup bearer by previous owners. That he has poured wine and served meals at banquets. Aren't you always on the lookout for serving boys who don't spill things?"

"Like everyone else, I prefer a serving lad who does not spill things, drop things and knock over the cups while I'm trying to eat. And he would look rather appealing going about such duties. Thanks for the suggestion, Mnester. Although, it is where you started."

"I haven't forgotten, Auntie Flavia," Mnester the dancer said.

CHAPTER 8

Flavia and Claudia decided to teach Marcius about clothes, make up and skin care as they considered themselves experts in those fields. After he was entirely well, Madam Falvia transferred Marcius to her most expensive brothel. Flavia considered her most exclusive house as a kind of private club for gentlemen. It was one of her favorite projects. There, she placed what she considered the cream of her crop, which were the best looking, most talented youths she owned. They came from various provinces.

Flavia's club was run by an employee, not a slave, called Clodia. Clodia was a poor Roman widow who was raising five sons in Rome's slums. Clodia had heard of Flavia's generosity and gone to her for a loan. Instead, she had given her a job. Flavia had insisted on meeting Clodia's sons while considering loaning Clodia some money and been impressed at the lads' obvious respect and devotion to their stern looking mother. In fact, while sharing some wine in Clodia's sparsely furnished, but spotless, apartment, Flavia had needed to stifle a laugh when Clodia smacked her eldest son when he was slow to do what his mother told him. As this son was well over twenty years of age, over six feet tall and a soldier, he had hardly felt the smack. But he grinned, rubbed his ear and said, "Mum! Not in front of guests."

His brothers laughed.

Flavia thought about it for a while and then said to Clodia, "You've raised some fine lads there. And if you can keep order amongst that bunch, you can keep order amongst my lads."

Flavia had to admit that order did need to be kept at her club. Flavia had some basic rules. She did not tolerate rudeness to the customers. On the other hand, no customer was allowed to abuse any of her lads either. Two burly, retired gladiators would firmly escort any difficult customer off the premises and dump him on the street in front of the house. Only very wealthy, powerful men could afford to go to Flavia's club, and they found this sort of treatment embarrassing and tried to avoid it.

One thing that really annoyed Flavia was if any of her slaves stole from a customer. She considered that a client's belongings should be safe in her club. It was bad for her business's reputation if her slaves stole things. If one of her lads was caught stealing, he would be rewarded with a smack across the ear. For a second offense, Flavia would tell one of her large bodyguards to switch her slave. If it happened again, the slave would be sold. Flavia also believed that stealing was unnecessary as each of the youths in her club received a proportion of what they earned each day, which was placed for them in their own locked strong box, which they had a key to, so they could spend or save their money as they chose.

Quarreling and fighting among the lads was more of a real problem as the youths did become bored and restless at times.

"Youthful high spirits," Flavia said.

"You're too soft with them," Clodia said.

Clodia handed out a few smacks and the occasional switching to discourage quarrels, and as she was a strong woman like Flavia, the youths took notice. With Abraham's help, Flavia kept an eye on her numerous businesses, but she was closely involved with her club. She trusted Clodia to run it efficiently, but she liked to drop in most evenings to see her favorite slaves and chat with the customers. When Marcius went to live there, he became the second fair boy in the house. There was a tall, solid, good natured German youth who became his friend very quickly. Marcius helped the German boy improve his Latin, for which the German lad was grateful. There were two Greek youths who would be best friends one minute, and shouting insults at each other in Greek the next. Sometimes they flew at each other. One of Flavia's doormen, repressing a grin, would separate them, hand out a few smacks, and they would settle down. There was an exquisitely languid Egyptian youth, and a clever Ethiopian with wonderful manners and a perfect body. They never caused any trouble.

But Flavia did not make Marcius start work immediately. She wanted him to look his best on his first night working in her club. So she rather enjoyed herself supervising her personal maid applying various lotions and oils to Marcius's body, face and hair. Her maid also advised Marcius on the best ways of removing most of his body hair. Flavia did not expect Marcius to remove his pubic hair as she wanted her clients to know Marcius was a natural blond. In fact, she did not require any of her slaves who worked in her brothels to remove their pubic hair. She considered it a dangerous and painful practice given the razors and creams then available in Rome. Flavia considered that her slaves were young men and women, not children. And as such they were all at least over the age of eighteen, therefore, they had body hair. If a client objected to this, they could go to someone else's brothels, in Madam Flavia's opinion.

She and Marcius discussed this issue one time as his body was massaged by a masseur. Every day he was massaged by a masseur and he rather enjoyed it. The rest of the beauty treatments Flavia insisted on he found dull, and he began to suspect that Madam Flavia had never owned a doll when she was a child, and was making up for lost time.

Flavia also called in a tailor who made Marcius four simple but stylish tunics in subtle colors and beautiful fabrics. The tailor was impressed at the instinct Falvia showed when choosing the clothes, which would bring out Marcius's looks. This tailor, Afer, made clothes for many of her slaves, and, although, in his opinion Madam Flavia tended to dress flamboyantly, she seemed to know instinctively what style of dress suited what style of person. When measuring Marcius, Afer thought, if she over paints him, and over dresses him, he'll look like any other boy tart in a cheap tavern. Flavia knows her business better than that.

Marcius was especially friendly with two other youths named Ptolemy and Beshar who worked in Flavia's brothel. They soon worked out that although he had been a cup bearer and a page boy that he had not worked as a prostitute in a brothel before. They tried to give him good advice. Soon after Marcius was given his own bedroom in the house, Ptolemy and Beshar took to visiting him in his room, sitting on his bed and chatting about different things. They explained the rules of the house and making suggestions about how he should behave with the customers.

In one of their earliest discussions, Ptolemy said to Marcius, "You don't have to anything you think sounds dangerous or disgusting. You say, 'No, we don't do that sort of thing here.' If the customer gets forceful about it, you call for help."

"Help?" Marcius asked.

"You'll have to say it louder than that, or Ruffio won't hear you," Beshar said with a grin.

"Which one of the doormen is Ruffio?" Marcius asked.

"The really big one," Ptolemy said.

"They're both huge. Are they from Thrace?" Marcius asked.

"How did you know that?" Ptolemy asked.

"I've met gladiators from Thrace before. I think there must be something in the water in the rivers in Thrace," Marcius said.

"You're not scared of them, are you, Marcius? I know they look scary, but that's just to intimidate the customers not us. They're paid to keep order but also protect us. And don't assume they can't move fast up the stairs. If you're in a difficult situation and you yell, they can bound up those stairs very quickly."

"But Ruffio punished Ariston a few days ago," Marcius commented.

"Ariston was caught with a valuable gold signet ring, which he stole from a customer. Auntie Flavia does not tolerate that sort of thing, and he's done it before. She gave him a choice between a switching and being sold. He decided on the switching. Mind you, he thought Auntie Falvia would do it, and she's not as strong as Ruffio," Ptolemy said.

Marcius looked at Ptolemy in surprise. He had assumed that Flavia would delegate the task of punishing one of her slaves to the doorman or the formidable Madam Clodia.

"Well, we do belong to her, Marcius," Ptolemy said. "And she does have a temper. We have to do what she and Auntie Clodia say. Madam Flavia punishes us sometimes if we break her rules, but she does not like doing it and she's usually sorry afterwards."

On his first evening officially working in the club, Marcius made a conquest without realizing it. One of Rome's generals, Quintas Marcellus Aquilus, had recently returned to Rome after a long tour of duty on the German frontier. Like most men in his position he had a wife, a family, but he also enjoyed regular visits to Flavia's club as he considered that she ran the best house in Rome and owned the most attractive professional boys in the city. Aquilus appreciated the fact that in Flavia's club he could expect to meet youths who were not only exceptionally good looking, but well mannered, intelligent and discrete. He also knew Flavia's reputation for genuinely caring for her employees' and slaves' health and welfare.

As the general went over to sit beside Madam Flavia and exchange greetings, he glanced around the room. Ptolemy and Ariston smiled politely at the general as he usually chose one of them to spend an hour or so with. Then Aquilus noticed the blond lad sitting beside Ptolemy. He could not help staring.

Now that is what I call a sweet looking boy, he thought.

He said to Madam Flavia, "The lad beside Ptolemy, is he new?"

"Yes," Flavia said. "This is his first night working for me, officially speaking."

"He's very fair. Is he a German lad?"

"No, he's from the north of Gaul," Flavia said.

"Are you serious? He's a Gaul? I never saw a Gaul who wasn't big, ugly and hairy."

"We're not all exactly the same," said Madam Flavia. "Some of us can be tamed and civilized," she added with considerable irony.

"How stupid of me, Madam Flavia. I forgot that you're originally from Gaul. I'm very sorry," Aquilus said.

"Well," she said. "It's a long time since I came to Rome. But, Marcius is new to Rome, and I have not owned him long. He's not experienced like some of my lads. But, he's a gentle sort of boy. He has a very sweet, affectionate nature which is very appealing."

"He certainly looks appealing, Flavia," Aquilus commented.

"Come here, Marcius," she said quietly.

Marcius quickly stood up and came over to the couch where his mistress and the General were seated. Flavia moved so that Marcius could sit between herself and Aquilus on her couch.

Now that he was sitting so close to him, the general could further appreciate Marcius's delicate skin and perfect features.

He also appreciated the delicate floral scent of Marcius's body and hair. Aquilus considered that some of Flavia's slave boys used too much make up and perfume, but he considered that Marcius had the balance right. Aquilus realized that Marcius had recently bathed and then used a small amount of makeup and scent, so he smelled fresh and clean.

Marcius filled the general's wine cup, then that of Madam Flavia.

"Have a cup yourself, Marcius," she said.

Aquilus lay back slightly on the couch and relaxed with his cup of wine in his hand. He looked at Marcius for a few more moments and then reached out with is other hand and put his arm around Marcius's narrow waist and encouraged him to lean back slightly as well. He liked that fact that Marcius seemed a little nervous and shy.

By this time, other customers were arriving and paying their respects to Madam Flavia. There was a certain procedure at Flavia's best brothel. Customers arrived, and the doormen helped them with their togas or cloaks, which were carefully hung up in the janitor's room beside the doors. Customers were then expected to greet Flavia and then were invited to sit beside whichever of her slaves they were interested in. Only wealthy, important men came to this brothel and most were aged in their thirties and forties. Most liked to sit and relax on the couches around Flavia's dining table, have some wine and snacks, talk with the slaves and their fellow guests before being led upstairs by the slave boy of their choice. Of course, on some evenings, the wine flowed freely, and a fair amount of petting, kissing and flirting occurred on the couches, but for anything beyond that, Flavia expected her boys to take their guests upstairs. Some customers found this odd at first, but Flavia's attitude was entirely practical.

"It is not hygienic to fuck in the same place where you eat. And how am I supposed to get the stains out of the couches later? And if Clodia is sitting in my place, and suddenly a sea of upright dicks appear, she might have a heart attack or something," Flavia said to her doormen one time.

Flavia was pleased with the way the general treated Marcius. Marcellus Aquilus was a regular visitor to her brothel when he was residing in Rome, and he always was pleasant to her slaves. His attitude when he put his arm around Marcius's waist to draw Marcius to him she considered gentle and encouraging. She thought Marcius so safe in this situation that she stood up and went to speak to other guests at her table.

As Marcellus Aquilus relaxed, he said to Marcius, "You're a beautiful boy. I'm sure you're going to please your mistress, and be very popular and successful."

"Madam Flavia is very good to me," Marcius said.

Marcellus Aquilus was surprised at the fluency of Marcius's Latin. He had assumed that Marcius's Latin would be very limited from what Flavia had told him of Marcius's origins.

"Your Latin is very good for a lad who has come to Rome recently," Aquilus said. "Where did you learn it?"

Marcius had prepared a story to cope with such questions.

"My father was a farmer and trader. He knew Roman and Greek traders, and he encouraged me to learn some Latin, so I could help him with his business in the future. But the war changed all that. Since I came to Rome, I have learned more Latin," Marcius said.

Aquilus did not press Marcius further for information about his past. As he had fought in Gaul, he could imagine the sort of things Marcius had seen and experienced during an eight year civil war when growing up. He knew why Marcius had been taken as a slave rather than killed. After the Roman army defeated an enemy tribe, the children and women of that tribe were usually enslaved rather than killed.

And any soldier with any brains at all, Marcellus Aquilus thought, when capturing a good looking lad like Marcius, would know he was worth more alive than dead.

Aquilus was not sure if he quite believed Marcius's story that his father had been some kind of merchant. He thought it more likely that a pretty blond boy like Marcius had been born to a pretty blond mother, who had been a prostitute or camp follower. Such origins would not prejudice Aquilus against Marcius. Aquilus had been a professional soldier all his adult life; he had survived wars across Europe and Asia, and he understood that civilians and captives had to do what they could to survive when their country has been occupied. In fact, he had quite a few fond memories of local women and youths in various countries who had been his companion for a short time when he was away from Rome. He had always treated his companions fairly.

He had sometimes irritated his fellow officers when commanding garrisons by ordering them to treat the local women with some decency. There was only so much he could do about the sexual behavior of the common soldiers, but he did tell his subordinate officers on one occasion, "Go to the local grog shops and pay for it. Plenty of the girls here will do it for a bracelet and a few coins. I am tired of outraged mothers turning up at my quarters; I have better things to do with my time. And yes, I am looking at you, Domitius Ahernobarbus."

So Marcellus Aquilus had no contempt in his attitude to someone like Marcius.

Once in Marcius's clean, comfortable room, Marcellus Aquilus started to remove his army uniform. Marcius went over to help him. Once he was more comfortable, Aquilus sat on the bed and leaned over to remove his sandals. Then he pulled his light undertunic up over his head, and removed his loincloth. As it was a warm evening, he lay back on the bed and got comfortable. He watched Marcius undress. Aquilus was a handsome man in his early forties. He was tall for a Roman, and he was very fit and well muscled due to his profession. Marcius admired Aquilus's body, but also he felt that Aquilus looked intelligent and good natured. As Marcius undressed he said to him, "I'd help you, but my big, rough soldier's hands might damage that pretty, new tunic you're wearing, and that would be a shame."

Once he was naked, Marcius turned his back to Aquilus so he could fold his tunic and other clothing neatly over the back of a chair. He placed his sandals under the chair.

"I wish my sons were neat like you, Marcius," Aquilus said.

But he was thinking that he had never seen such a fine looking back and buttocks. Now that Marcius no longer belonged to Atellus, he no longer had bruises or red stripes on his body. And the beauty treatments and massage that Flavia had made him endure, by this time, meant that his skin and hair looked perfect.

He could model for a sculptor, Aquilus thought. But if the sculptor liked boys, I'm not sure how much actual sculpting would get done.

Marcius slid into bed beside the naked Roman general, who immediately opened his arms, so he could cuddle Marcius. He was being considerate, but he could tell that Marcius was nervous.

"Are you frightened of me, Marcius?" he asked.

"No, sir," Marcius said. "I'm nervous because this is my first night working for the madam."

"Yes, she told me you're very new to this kind of work. I understand, Marcius. And she understands that you're not like some of the boys she owns. I'm a straight forward sort of man; do your best to please me. I can't expect more than that," Aquilus said.

"Thank you, sir," Marcius said.

As Marcius rested his head on the general's chest, Aquilus reached over with his right hand to touch and run his fingers through Marcius long fair hair. He was pleased to discover that not only was Marcius's hair of such a beautiful golden color, but that it was also very fine, soft, sweet smelling and abundant. And as Aquilus stroked his hair, Marcius lay on his chest and he relaxed as he had always found it soothing when someone brushed or stroked his hair especially near his hairline, although the last person to do so had probably been his mother when he was a child. Aquilus stroked Marcius's hairline, and, if Marcius were a cat, he would have been purring by this stage.

"You like that, do you?" Aquilus asked.

"I always have," Marcius said. "When I was ill when I was little, my mother used to stroke my hair. It always sent me to sleep."

"Me, too," said Aquilus. "But don't tell anyone I said that. My soldiers might lose respect for me."

"Don't they know you are a mortal? Or do Roman soldiers think all their generals are gods?" Marcius asked.

"You're being cheeky, Marcius," Aquilus said but he could not help grinning.

"Am I? I didn't mean to be, sir," Marcius said.

"Perhaps not. And it's a good question," Aquilus said.

And it shows that this barbarian, this captive, this slave prostitute, actually looks around him and thinks about things, he thought.

He continued to stroke Marcius's hair. As he cuddled and stroked such a beautiful and pleasing youth his penis had started to stiffen. Marcius reached out and stroked Aquilus's penis before gently touching his testicles with his fingertips. If Aquilus's penis was not very long, it was certainly thick, and his testicles were large. Marcius gently took hold of Aquilus's semi-erect penis and started to manipulate it to bring him to a full erection.

He might hurt me a bit, Marcius thought. But he would not intend to. He's not mean like that.

Such a nice gentle touch, Aquilus thought.

Once Aquilus was fully erect, he spread his legs wide, and Marcius moved to position himself kneeling between his legs and bending over to take the general's erect penis into his mouth. Marcius licked and sucked in the way he thought Aquilus would enjoy.

As Marcius moved up and down, he watched the long blond hair cascade over his belly and thighs. Aquilus reached down to caress Marcius's hair and encourage him.

"So nice, Marcius. So gentle and loving," he whispered.

He considered if Marcius was not as expert sexually as Ptolemy or Flavia's slaves like Demetrios and Ariston he was certainly pleasing.

When he was ready, Aquilus asked Marcius to lie on his stomach on the bed. Marcius quickly did so and spread his legs so the general could kneel between them.

"Where's some ointment?" Aquilus asked.

Marcius reached under the bed and handed a ceramic jar with lubricating ointment in it. The general started to gently apply the ointment to Marcius's bottom; both externally and internally. Although Marcius by this time was more used to being penetrated by this time, he could not help cringing as Aquilus's finger entered him.

Flavia was not joking, Aquilus thought. This lad is no slut.

He coated his penis with the ointment, then stroked Marcius's bottom a few times.

"Try to relax. I can see that you're not like some boys. I'll do my best not to hurt you," he commented.

Aquilus did not really hurt Marcius. By now, Marcius had learned not to think during sex and his body responded automatically. It was easier not to think about what was happening as the general did not really require Marcius to do much except stay reasonably still while he thrust inside him. Aquilus rested briefly after his climax but managed to keep most of his weight off Marcius. Then he withdrew and rested on the other side of the bed. When he opened his eyes he saw that Marcius had turned his face to him on the pillow and was looking at him.

"I hope I did not hurt you, Marcius," Aquilus said.

"No sir. It felt fine," Marcius said.

"Fine?" Aquilus said with a smile. "I appreciate your honesty, Marcius."

Unlike some men, Aquilus did not expect to be flattered by a sexual partner. In fact, he found it irritating when on occasions prostitutes told him what a wonderful, skilled lover he was. He wondered if any man seriously believed such talk from a prostitute.

Aquilus got up and found a pitcher and basin on a table so he could wash. Then he dressed. Marcius watched him as he did so. Aquilus said to Marcius, "You're a lovely lad, Marcius. I intend to see you again in the future."

"I'd like that, too, sir," Marcius said.

Marcius then washed, dressed and returned to the brothel's reception area while Aquilus went to Flavia's office and paid her. As he was a regular visitor he knew how many silver coins to pay the madam. But he reached into his pouch and found two gold coins which he gave her for Marcius. He knew that Flavia's slaves received a share of what they earned as well as any extra coins or small gifts from customers.

"He's an exceptional lad, Flavia. And I don't just mean because of his looks; he's so gentle and eager to please. I'm sure he's going to be an asset to this house."

"I think so, too, general," Flavia said.

Later, Flavia returned to her couch and whispered to Marcius.

"Did Marcellus Aquilus treat you properly?"

"Yes, Auntie Flavia. He seems a pleasant person."

"None of my lads have ever complained to me about him, although Ptolemy says he's not exactly inventive sexually speaking," Flavia said.

"I don't mind that," Marcius said. "It's his money; he should get what he wants."

"You're right, Marcius," said Flavia.

Marcius spent an hour or so with other customers that afternoon and evening, but Flavia saw to it that she only introduced him to men she knew something about. She made it her business to know how customers behaved once they were alone with one of her lads. As Flavia had been a prostitute herself when younger she knew how a client who seemed pleasant and ordinary enough in conversation could suddenly turn violent or behave oddly once alone with a slave. Flavia knew most of the men who came regularly to this house, but she always made sure that any new client was discretely observed by herself, Clodia or her doormen.

Over the next few weeks, Marcius was popular with clients. In fact, her business continued to thrive as rumors about an exquisite sweet, new blond boy at Flavia's club circulated. Ariston and Demetrious resented this, especially when some clients whom they considered their regulars chose Marcius instead of one of them.

"Don't be silly," Ptolemy said to them when they grumbled. "He's the new boy and people are curious about him. And you know how some men are about blonds. Your regulars will come back to you."

Ptolemy proved to be correct. Although everyone agreed Marcius was lovely to look at, the customers who preferred experienced dark youths like himself and the Greeks soon returned to them. Beshar and Henguist were least affected by Marcius's brief period of such popularity, as they were more boyish than the other boys in the house. The men they attracted, although they looked at Marcius appreciatively, preferred to spend their time with more masculine lads like Beshar and Henguist.

CHAPTER 9

After the first months, when Flavia and her accountant were going through her records, Flavia noticed that although Ariston and Demetrious were earning the most for her, Ptolemy and Marcius were making quite a lot of money, too.

"At this rate," Abraham Ben Joseph said. "He'll be able to buy his freedom from you in no time."

"Yes," she said. "That's what worries me."

"Pardon?"

"What is he going to do afterwards? How is he going to make a living? It's not like he has been trained in any occupation," Flavia said.

"You'll find some sort of work for him later. In your house or one of your businesses. He's literate, bright and honest. Or he may decide to go home to Gaul."

"Yes, there's that of course," Flavia said.

After Flavia felt that Marcius had settled in she left more of the day to day responsibilities of running her club to Clodia, although Clodia made regular reports to Flavia. During one of these reports she asked Flavia suddenly, "Don't you mind that the boys sleep with each other?"

"They're young men," said Flavia with a grin. "What do you expect? As long as they're not tired when the customers arrive, I don't care. That hasn't happened, has it?" Flavia asked.

"No," Clodia admitted.

"I didn't think so. They're professionals; my best boys. Try not to be a prude, Clodia. In this business, you can't be. Is Marcius better now?"

"He got over that cold or whatever it was. He's back at work and popular with the customers," Clodia said.

"Don't make him work too hard," Flavia said.

"Of course not. I know he's not that strong," Clodia said.

"How does he get on with the other boys?" Flavia asked.

"Fine. The German boy is his best friend. The Greeks are jealous, but you know what they're like. And, the Egyptian is in love with him," Clodia said.

"Really? Are they a couple?" Flavia asked.

"Well. Every time I send for Ptolemy he seems to be dozing in Marcius's bed. So I assume they're together."

Flavia was quiet for a moment.

"You do approve, don't you? Ptolemy has such a sweet nature, and Marcius could do with some affection."

"Yes, he needs someone to care for him. And Ptolemy is very loving, isn't he? I think he'll be good for Marcius."

Ptolemy was good for Marcius. All the youths had experiences in their past, which they preferred to forget and appreciated customers who were pleasant. But, they knew not to become emotionally involved with customers. When they needed affection they turned to each other. Flavia and Clodia also tended to act maternally when needed. Ptolemy had fallen for Marcius as soon as he entered the house, and, in his quiet way, set about seducing him. It had not been that difficult as Ptolemy was as exquisitely beautiful as Marcius, except that he was dark not fair, and, sexually speaking, one of Flavia's most talented slaves. Ptolemy was also compassionate, and he listened when Marcius needed to talk. Marcius sometimes had nightmares, would wake up and cry out. He often dreamed that he was back chained in Atellus's cellar and Atellus and his friends were coming down the stairs to hurt and humiliate him. Marcius would wake terrified. Ptolemy, who slept in the room next room, would quietly slip into Marcius's room and bed and sooth him. Sometimes, Marcius just needed to be held. Marcius could cry in front of Ptolemy and not be embarrassed about it later. Marcius felt that Ptolemy understood him and he did as Ptolemy had belonged to a cruel master in the past.

"They must look lovely together," Flavia said.

"They do," said Clodia. "I have to send a bodyguard out with them every time they leave the house."

"Why?"

"They keep being followed home by gladiators," Clodia said.

"Only a champion gladiator could afford one of my lads," Flavia said.

CHAPTER 10

After a few weeks working in Flavia's club, an event occurred, which led to rumors circulating throughout the city concerning Marcius. One day, in the early afternoon when Flavia and Clodia where organizing the household before clients where expected to arrive, there was a determined knocking on the door. As usual, Ruffio opened the door. He found a strangely dressed but Latin speaking young man. Behind this man was some other men including a tall, solid man who in Roman opinion would be considered over dressed, over groomed, wearing an outrageously colorful tunic and far too many jewels. Standing either side of the individual were two massive slaves who were obviously bodyguards. Behind them was a small group of younger well dressed men.

"Good afternoon," the man at the door said politely. "Is this the house of Madam Falvia?"

"Yes."

"My master, Prince Perseus, has been told that Madam Flavia runs the best establishment of this kind in Rome, and he wishes to pay his respects to the lady," the spokesman said.

"I'll tell her your master is here. I'm sure she will want to greet the gentleman personally," Ruffio said. He closed the door, and then almost ran to Flavia's office.

"Is the house on fire?" Flavia asked as Ruffio burst through the doorway.

"There's some sort of Eastern monarch with an entourage at the front door. He looks like the Great King of Persia to me, and from the look on his face, I think he's got a stiffy," Ruffio said.

"Well, I better welcome him in person then," she said.

As Flavia and Ruffio hurried to the door, Flavia could not resist teasing Ruffio.

"If he really is a Persian king, Ruffio, and he fancies you, you'll just have to grit your teeth and put up with it," she said.

"Not much chance of that," Ruffio said.

Prince Perseus was not actually a king, or even a Persian, but he was very rich and the ruler of a strategically placed Eastern country, and he was negotiating a treaty with Julius Caesar. But, even a prince of an Eastern country has to relax sometimes. At a fairly dull official dinner party in his honor, another guest, who was sitting beside him, noticed the way the prince looked at the attractive slave boys serving the meal. So, he said quietly to the prince, "If you wish to meet the best, professional Greek lads in Rome, go to the house of Madam Flavia. It's expensive, but worth it."

When Prince Perseus seemed interested, the Roman gave him detailed instructions to the house. So, the next afternoon, Prince Perseus set out on foot with his interpreter, some of his favorite nobles, and two massive bodyguards. (This, for him, was a small entourage). Madam Flavia welcomed him warmly into her establishment, and the prince, in a friendly manner, sat beside her on her couch. He then gestured to his interpreter who sat the other side to Flavia. His nobles then seated themselves on various couches around the table, as Clodia and Flavia's other doorman, Gazno, brought cups, jugs and pitchers of wine from the kitchen. Clodia hurried back to the kitchen to assemble some platters and bowls of snacks for the customers. Flavia's establishment did not provide meals, as such, but she always provided snacks for customers. Flavia had lived long enough to know that when her guests drank her wine in the afternoons and evenings, it was a good idea if they ate something at the same time. As she talked to the prince, her slaves started to come into the dining room. It had not taken long for most of them to get downstairs, as when Flavia had gone to the front door to greet the prince and his people,

Clodia had run to the base of the staircase and shouted, "Boys! Get down here. Customers! Now!"

As usual, Henguist and Beshar the Ethiopian arrived first as they only had to neaten their tunics, and put a comb through their hair before coming downstairs. The Greeks, Demetrios and Ariston, arrived next, but they had paused to apply some make up and perfume. Marcius arrived after them. He, too, had stopped to neaten his tunic, hair and apply a little make up. Ptolemy arrived last. Flavia understood this and did not mind. Ptolemy did his make up in the Egyptian fashion, which Flavia knew was more time consuming than the style in which the Greek youths and Marcius used make up. Besides, Ptolemy had a way of making an entrance into her dining room; he seemed to glide into the room rather than simply walking through the door way followed closely by his Egyptian cat called Mau.

Ptolemy's cat was a frequent cause of dispute between Flavia and Clodia. Flavia loved all animals and kept numerous pets in her home and at some of her other houses. At that time, not many Romans kept cats as pets, although ships from Egypt and Phoenicia brought them in and sold them as exotic pets to upper class fashionable Romans. Ptolemy's cat had been given to him as a present by a Phoenician merchant who owned his own fleet of ships and who bought her as a present for Ptolemy in Egypt. This cat was most attached to Ptolemy and Marcius, but accepted pats and snacks from the other inhabitants. The only person in the house who did not much care for the cat was Clodia.

"What's the matter with having a cat in the house?" Flavia asked her one day.

"I have to clean up after her," Clodia muttered.

"You clean up after the guard dogs without complaining and they have a lot more 'accidents' than she does. She's very fussy about cleanliness and she keeps mice and rats away from the kitchen."

"I don't like the way she stares at me, as if she knows everything I'm thinking," Clodia said.

"A cat would look at an emperor or a pharaoh like that according to Ptolemy. Besides, he loves her and it's someone he can talk his own language to," Flavia said.

Once the youths were seated on the couches in pairs, Prince Perseus gestured to his nobles to seat themselves on the couches. Two nobles went over and sat beside Demetrios and Ariston and started to speak to them in Greek. Marcius and Ptolemy (and Ptolemy's cat) sat together on a couch and the prince looked at them while he chatted and had a cup of wine with Flavia. He was trying to make up his mind. When Marcius said something to Ptolemy and then smiled, the prince decided.

There are exquisite Egyptian lads back home, he thought. But not lovely blond lads like that one.

He took from his belt a pouch and handed it to the madam. Flavia opened it to see it was full of gold coins.

"I would like a night with one of your lads," he said. "And a lad for each of my companions, of course."

"Of course, sir," Flavia said.

The prince then nodded to his bodyguards who sat beside Henguist and Beshar. This surprised Flavia, and it must have showed on her face as the prince smiled and commented, "A loyal slave deserves moments of pleasure and relaxation, too. I'm sure you agree, madam."

"I do," she said.

One thing about this prince, she thought, he's no snob.

"Which of my lads?" she asked.

"It's not an easy decision to make," he said. "All of your lads are lovely, each in his own distinct way. But, perhaps, that fair lad with the lovely smile would like to come over and sit beside me."

"Of course," Flavia said.

Marcius came over and the interpreter stood up and made room for him on the couch. The interpreter looked somewhat at a loss until Ptolemy smiled invitingly at him. So the interpreter went to sit next to Ptolemy, spoke to him in Egyptian, and stroked his cat. Ptolemy beamed with pleasure at being addressed in his own language.

"Is your interpreter Egyptian?" Flavia asked.

"He's something of a mixture; he has Egyptian, Greek and Roman blood," the prince said.

"That has to be a great start in life for someone who becomes an interpreter," Flavia commented.

As Flavia and the prince chatted, Prince Perseus encouraged Marcius to sit on his lap. Flavia wisely did not talk about politics, but chatted to the foreign prince about his impressions of Rome and suggested sights and entertainments that he and his nobles might like to see while visiting Rome. Marcius did not interrupt their conversation and only spoke when invited to by Flavia or the prince. Prince Perseus thought this appropriate behavior for someone of Marcius's age and status.

Flavia glanced at Ariston and Demetrios who seemed to be enjoying the attentions of the two Greek speaking nobles. She glanced at Behar and Henguist who she rightly imagined had no common language with the prince's bodyguards. But the four men seemed to be communicating mainly through gestures, touch and appeared to admiring each other's well toned and well muscled bodies. Flavia nodded at Beshar who took his admirer's hand and stood up to lead upstairs to his room. Henguist did the same. The Greeks chatted for a while before leading their customers upstairs. But the prince was in no particular hurry to take Marcius upstairs. He had paid for the whole night, and he genuinely found Madam Flavia an interesting person to talk to. After a while, Flavia faked a half yawn behind her hand. The prince took the hint. "I think it's time I took this man to his bed. The young need their rest," he said with considerable irony.

Later, the prince considered that he had chosen well. Apart from his good looks, Prince Perseus admired Marcius's gentle, polite, quiet manner, and what seemed to him, a genuine desire to please and satisfy him. The prince was a sensuous person and a very experienced lover, and as he was in no hurry, he took his time caressing and massaging Marcius's beautiful young body until Marcius was very aroused. By the time the prince entered him from the side, Marcius was very willing and responsive.

The prince woke Marcius two more times in the night to touch him and enjoy him. Marcius was surprised at Prince Perseus's stamina for a man aged in his thirties.

"I suppose he's entitled to get his money's worth," he commented to Ptolemy later.

After the prince and Marcius had gone upstairs, Flavia glanced at the only two people left in her dining room, Ptolemy and the interpreter who were chatting pleasantly. She nodded at Ptolemy, which meant that he was to take the interpreter up to his room. She then went to the kitchen to find Clodia.

"Have they gone upstairs yet? Should I clear the table?" Clodia asked.

"I'll do it," Flavia said. "You're looking tired."

As Clodia did not argue with her, she realized that Clodia was indeed tired. But the time Flavia returned to the dining room her faithful doormen, Ruffio and Ganzo were collecting platters, bowls, cups and jugs from the table and taking them to the kitchen. Between the three of them, tidying up the dining room was quickly done. In the kitchen, they decided to leave the dishes until the next day although Clodia objected to this. Flavia told her to go home with Ganzo as her escort as night had fallen by this time.

"I can look after myself," Clodia said huffily.

"The streets are dangerous for anyone at this time of night," Flavia said sensibly.

As Clodia and Ganzo left, Ruffio turned to Flavia, and said, "Should I lock up the house now?"

"As soon as Ganzo gets back. I'll need both of you to stay tonight. With so many strangers in the house staying until morning, I don't want my lads unprotected."

"Or the coins in your strong box in the office," Ruffio said with a cheeky grin.

"That, too," Flavia said.

After locking up the house, Ruffio did a quick check upstairs to see that everything was relatively peaceful. This was a part of his job. He considered that his job was to protect the madam and her lads. He, therefore, when at work only drank water. He knew to deal with any trouble, he needed to be sober, alert, calm and use his excellent hearing. Admittedly, when he and Ganzo were not working, they went to taverns together, but they were moderate drinkers by anyone's standards. They favored taverns where the food was good and the company cheerful. There, they spent more time eating, talking and gambling than actually drinking. If Ruffio had a weakness (and who does not?) it was for gambling. But as Flavia knew his worth and paid him a decent salary as a result, he did not see his gambling as a problem. On occasions, Ruffio's wife took a different view, but that's a different story.

After counting the gold coins given to her by the prince, she returned them to their pouch and locked them securely in her strong box. Then she went to sleep on the couch in her office. She would have been more comfortable in her own bed in her home, but it was late, she had drunk more than she usually did when chatting to the prince, and she was tired. Despite this, she woke reasonably early and went to the kitchen to find that Ruffio and Ganzo were making a start on the dishes. She found a cloth and started to dry the dishes.

"Clodia not here yet?" she asked.

"We thought we'd make a start on cleaning up. Mind you, she'll tell us we haven't cleaned things thoroughly, and put everything away in the wrong place," Ganzo commented.

"Well, at least we tried, and did not just leave a mess for her to clean up by herself," Flavia commented.

"What about some breakfast for the lads?" Ruffio asked.

"Yes. They'll be hungry as usual. And for our guests; it would be rude not to offer them a decent breakfast after all the money they've spent," Flavia said.

"I could boil up some porridge," Ganzo said.

"I will not insult my guests like that," Flavia said.

Despite having lived in Rome for over twenty years, Flavia usually described the wheat porridge which sustained most of Rome's population as "the sort of sludge I would not feed to a pig, unless I particularly disliked the pig".

So, Flavia boiled eggs and fried bacon; Ruffio sliced bread and cheese. Ganzo found olives in jars and enough fresh fruit to fill two bowls.

"And we'll need some jugs of water and cups. Everyone this morning will appreciate a cup of cool, fresh water; me for a start," Flavia said.

By the time the prince, his entourage and Flavia's slaves were heading down the stairs, a simple, but plentiful breakfast was set out on the table. It was a relaxed, informal meal where people helped themselves and passed each other bowls and platters. Everyone ate some fruit and drank water, most ate bread, cheese and olives. Those present with really good appetites like the prince, his bodyguards and Flavia's German slave, Henguist, appreciated the bacon and eggs.

If eating was a sporting event, Flavia thought, Henguist could eat for Germania and win a gold medal. Flavia then looked at Marcius and was immediately concerned. Prince Perseus started to say something to her and noticed the worried look on her face. He looked in Marcius's direction and saw what was wrong. On Marcius's plate there was only a small bunch of grapes and a small pear.

She worries that Marcius does not eat enough, the prince thought. She loves him like her own child.

After his night with Marcius, he had thought of asking if Flavia would consider selling Marcius to him.

I would be wasting my breath, he thought.

The prince could also imagine just how the ladies of his household would react if he brought to his palace a pretty boy from Rome as his cup bearer. His chief wife, who was the daughter of a king and the mother of his three eldest adult sons, would complain to her father, her brother, her sons and then attempt to nag him to death. His favorite concubine (at the moment) would throw tantrums and, perhaps, a few valuable vases around. As she was no fool, she would not throw them at the prince, but she would make her feelings known, at considerable volume, to everyone in his household.

Yes, he's pretty and sweet, but not worth uproar in my household, the prince concluded.

So, at the end of the meal, he stood up, took Flavia's hand and kissed the back of it.

"I must compliment you on the way you organize a party at short notice, Madam Flavia. Many of Rome's high born ladies could take lessons from you when it comes to seeing to the comfort of their guests," he said.

"Why? Thank you, sir," she said.

Then the prince and his entourage left. As soon as they were gone, Flavia smiled at her slaves and said, "Boys. We all deserve some time off. As soon as you've bathed come to the office, and I'll give you some spending money. Go and enjoy yourselves, but be back by nightfall."

Soon after Flavia was handed out silver coins to her lads. Ruffio, Ganzo and Henguist went to the chariot races where they placed modest bets, lost some money but won enough to go to a tavern for a meal and some drinks. Demetrious and Ariston went to the markets and treated themselves to small luxuries like sweets, perfume and trinkets. Ptolemy went to a store where he bought papyrus, charcoal, paint and paint brushes. Ptolemy designed and made jewelry as a hobby. His father had been a jeweler in Alexandria, and Ptolemy had briefly been his apprentice. Ptolemy intended to earn his freedom and continue in his father's trade in Rome. Marcius went to bookseller and purchased two second hand scrolls; some poetry in Latin, and a short play in Greek. With the help of his tutor, Marcius now read Latin very well, but he had decided that he needed to know more Greek. His tutor was delighted at teaching Greek to such a bright, enthusiastic student. Even Demetrious and Ariston, having got over their jealousy of Marcius, would speak Greek with him, if they were in the right mood, that is.

As Ptolemy started a new design in his room, Marcius lay on his bed and read. The Greek play was a little difficult for him, so he set it aside intending to get his tutor to help him with it at his next lesson.

He had no difficulty reading the Latin poetry. After midday Marcius had a nap. Flavia often noticed how tired Marcius appeared some days and had him examined by no less than three different doctors. But they all told her similar things.

"I see no sign of a serious illness or problem," Falvia's own doctor said. "He is simply not a robust person. He will always need to look after his health; he should eat more, drink less and take more exercise such as walking and swimming."

"You doctors say that to everyone," Flavia said.

"Because it's good advice for practically everyone," the doctor said with a smile.

But because he was a friend as well as a doctor, he added, "Try not to worry about Marcius. He does rest and read when he's unwell. That shows common sense and patience for such a young man. He told me he was often ill as a child especially in winter."

"And winters are harsh in the north of Gaul. Usually only the toughest babies survive," Flavia said.

"His mother must have loved him very much," the doctor said. "And now he has you to look after him."

Madam Flavia and Madam Clodia spent their free time at their respective homes with their families.

The brothel was so quiet in the late afternoon that Ptolemy thought he was alone until he heard Marcius playing the flute in his room. Later Ptolemy and Marcius went to the kitchen to prepare themselves a simple meal. Demetrious and Ariston returned at dusk as they knew that they would not be safe out on the streets after dark. They had spent some time in the markets but also some time in a tavern where they ate, drank and danced to music from their homeland. They also flirted outrageously with good looking young soldiers, sailors and gladiators. If Flavia had known of this she would have been seriously annoyed. She would have smacked the pair of them and said, "You're supposed to be highly paid professionals, so stop giving it away to any good looking man who asks you."

Demetrious and Ariston retired to Ariston's room fairly early after chatting to Marcius and Ptolemy briefly. Marcius and Ptolemy also went to bed early. The house was quiet until Ruffio, Ganzo and Henguist arrived back at the house. They did not worry about thugs roaming the streets after dark.

"We are the thugs roaming the streets," Ruffio commented to Ganzo that evening.

The three had enjoyed their day and evening away from the house, but only Henguist could be considered truly drunk. But as Henguist was as good natured drunk as he was sober; his companions did not mind making sure that he arrived back at the brothel safely. Henguist, in fact, was drunk enough to sing a rude song in German as they approached the brothel's back door. It was just as well that none of Flavia's neighbors knew any German, or Flavia would have received complaints the next day. But Ruffio and Ganzo simply grinned, steered Henguist through the doorway, up the stairs, and into his bed. Henquist fell asleep almost immediately. Ruffio grinned at Ganzo.

"Germans and Gauls are exactly the same when it comes to drinking. You put a flagon in front of them and they think they have to down it in a few seconds and call out for the next one."

"That's how they drink where they come from," said Ganzo.

"It can't be good for their health," Ruffio said.

"Health?" Ganzo asked. "The other thing that would affect Henguist's health would be if a building collapsed on him, and even then, it would have to be a big building."

"I wasn't thinking of Henguist or Madam Flavia. I've seen her drink most Romans under the table. But she and Henguist are strong and healthy. Little Marcius should not drink the way he does. He's delicate to start with, and drinking will only make him more prone to illness."

CHAPTER 11

General Aquilus soon heard rumors at the public baths about a new blond at Madam Flavia's club. In fact, he overheard someone at the baths say, "A Syrian king paid a chest of gold for one night with a pretty new German lad she owns."

A chest of gold for one night? Aquilus wondered. A German lad? Henquist? Marcius? No, it's not possible.

Aquilus was a methodical man. By this time spending some time in the late afternoon with Marcius or Ptolemy had become part of his daily routine. He would conduct any business he needed to do in the mornings, have a snack near midday and then go to the baths in the afternoon. On the way to his home for dinner, he would stop at Flavia's club for an hour or so. So the next time he went to the brothel, he said to the madam, "What's this about a Syrian king paying a chestful of gold for one night with one of your German lads?"

Once she stopped laughing, Flavia said, "Don't you love rumors, General. There always contain just a tiny element of the truth, but that's all. The man was a prince not a king, he certainly wasn't Syrian, and it was a pouch of gold coins not a chest. He also paid for his nobles to have one of my lads, too. And Marcius is not from Germania, he's from the north of Gaul like me. But don't tell anyone that, General. Rumors like that are wonderful for business. All Rome is gossiping about my little Marcius. He's famous now, or, should I say, notorious? Marcius is going to be quite a success."

"I hope you're not going to charge me that sort of price to see Marcius," the general said.

"Of course not, General. That was an unusual situation. I charge the same for all my lads. It only leads to jealousy and bickering if I don't. Of course, if a customer wishes to give one of the boys a few coins extra or a little present that's fine with me," Flavia said.

Aquilus continued his regular visits at Flavia's club. He was always pleasant to Marcius. He certainly did not ask Marcius about his past. For the general, seeing someone like Marcius on a regular basis was a solution to a problem. At that time, he and his wife no longer shared a bed due to his wife's ill health. They both regarded this as a temporary arrangement. His wife had experienced a difficult childbirth the previous year and had been in poor health since. Various doctors had warned him that another pregnancy too soon might kill her. His wife had had difficulties in her previous pregnancies. The general was the father of four surviving children, which he considered quite sufficient. A more callous man might have divorced his wife and married again, but he loved and respected his wife, he loved his children, and he enjoyed his comfortable well run home. He did not blame his wife for the fact that she was obviously fertile but had difficulties when pregnant and when giving birth.

I'm the idiot who kept getting her pregnant every time I came home on leave, he told himself one time. As an alternative, he could have kept a mistress in a small flat somewhere, but he had done that sort of thing in the past and found himself quarreling with both his wife and his mistress on regular occasions once they found out about each other. By seeing Marcius regularly, Aquilus fulfilled his sexual needs without disrupting his well organized routine. He did not expect anything more from Marcius than that. Once Aquilus got into the habit of seeing Marcius most afternoons, after a few weeks he realized that Marcius was not only a beauty, but also good company. Although Aquilus did not confide in him the way he would when talking to his wife, a family member, or close friends, he found that Marcius was capable of interesting and amusing conversations. Aquilus discovered that Marcius had a rather dry sense of humor, which he appreciated. Although Aquilus's attitude was that he did not go to a brothel for a conversation, after he and Marcius had made love, he would spend some time dozing or lying in Marcius's bed, and they would talk about topics such as Marcius's studies, music, plays and entertainments he had been to, and anything odd or amusing that had happened in the household. In short, the general could relax and feel comfortable in Marcius's company.

CHAPTER 12

There was one problem that concerned Clodia, which she raised with Flavia.

"Marcius drinks too much," she said. "And, after a few drinks, he says things he shouldn't."

"He's insolent?" Flavia asked.

"Not exactly. He has an odd sense of humor. Sometimes he makes comments which are funny, but he goes too far. I wouldn't mind so much except that sometimes he's cheeky to me in front of the other lads, and, since you won't let me discipline him ..."

Flavia interrupted.

"He's had enough discipline," she said.

"I'm only talking about a slap. All boys his age need a smack now and again. They get too big for their boots otherwise," Clodia said. "You let me punish the other boys."

"Marcius is a special case. Any trouble, and I'll deal with it," Flavia said.

But, Flavia did start to worry about Marcius's drinking after talking to him one afternoon. As a fellow Gaul who, in her younger days, could drink most Romans under the table, she had assumed that Clodia had been worrying unnecessarily. But, even she noticed how fast Marcius could empty an amphora.

Clodia had said to her, "He's never too drunk to work. It's just that some afternoons he's never really drunk, but he's never really sober either."

That sounds like Atellus, Flavia thought.

Then she realized that Atellus would have given Marcius wine regularly. It would have made him even more dependent on him. Flavia knew how Atellus worked. Marcius would have been given decent food, wine, and decent living conditions if he had been a good boy and done everything his master told him to do, and a merciless thrashing if he displeased him. And wine would have helped Marcius cope with the pain and fear he must have felt during that time. It would have offered him a temporary escape from an awful present reality. But Flavia did not want Marcius to drink too much as she knew it was not good for him. Flavia was vaguely aware she controlled her slaves through rewards and punishments as Porcius Atellus did, but she preferred to reward rather than punish, and any punishments she handed out were not excessive or undeserved.

Flavia decided to speak to Marcius about his drinking. Thinking about it later, she knew she had not gone about it the right way. She should have called him to Clodia's office and spoken to him calmly and privately. Instead, one afternoon, in front of Clodia, customers and the other youths she snapped at him, "Don't throw my wine down your throat so fast. I don't pay you to get drunk and disgusting."

As he had drunk quite a few cups of wine he muttered, "You pay me to be disgusting."

"Disgusting is what you do best, pretty boy. And you weren't exactly a virgin when I bought you," Flavia snapped back.

"At least I'm not an over painted old whore," Marcius sneered.

This attitude to Flavia was too insulting for her to tolerate. Everyone stared at the madam. Flavia knew she could not permit Marcius to speak to her like that, so she calmly put down her own cup of wine, stood up, walked over to Marcius and gave him as stinging slap across the face. Like Clodia, when she put her heart and soul into it, not to mention, her powerful right arm behind it, Flavia could administer a hard slap. Marcius looked appalled and started to apologize but Flavia shushed him and ordered him to Clodia's office to wait for her.

"He's for a flogging," a customer whispered to another customer.

"Madam Flavia won't be too harsh. That boy is rather special to her," said Aquilus. Aquilus genuinely liked Marcius, but he had noticed Marcius's tendency to make comments to Madam Clodia without thinking about it first. He had seen him get away with this before, but he had never seen him insult Madame Flavia. By the time Flavia entered the office, Marcius was frightened. Flavia sat on a chair opposite him and looked at him as she picked up the switch that was kept in the office. Marcius looked at Flavia.

"I'm sorry, Auntie Flavia. I deserve a thrashing," he said humbly.

"Yes, Marcius. You do. Do you know what you've done wrong?" she asked.

"I was insulting and insolent," Marcius said.

"And?" Flavia prompted.

"And ... ungrateful," he said. "You treat me well. You saved me from Atellus."

"So you shouldn't insult me, should you?" Flavia said.

"No, mistress," he said.

"Marcius. I cannot tolerate insolence from you, especially in front of the others. You boys would walk all over me if I did that," Flavia said.

"I know," Marcius said. "What are you going to do to me?"

"I could sell you to someone like Atellus perhaps. He's not exactly the only cruel master in Rome."

"Please don't do that, Auntie Flavia," Marcius begged. "Madam Clodia or Ruffio could beat me if you don't want to do it."

Ruffio was Flavia's biggest, toughest bodyguard. She and Marcius both knew that he would give Marcius quite a thrashing and consider that he thoroughly deserved it.

"No Marcius," she said. "It's my responsibility."

So Marcius meekly bent over the desk and Flavia caned his bottom about ten times. She hit him hard enough to make him cry out as she wanted the other youths to hear. It was quiet in the other room. The youths winced as they heard the blows being delivered, and poor Ptolemy was in tears for his friend. Marcius wept as he sat down on a stool. Flavia put down the cane and went over to him. She hugged him to her motherly bosom and tried to calm down herself. She stroked his lovely blond hair.

"There, there, little Gaul. I'm sorry, but I had to do it. It's all finished now. It's all over. Now, try to stop crying and go wash your face. You're ruining your looks and the general is probably waiting for you. I would not usually make you work now, but he has been waiting a fair while for you, and I don't wish to offend him."

Marcius nodded miserably. After washing his face, Marcius tried to calm down by taking some deep breathes. He knew he had to control himself before going to a customer. As he entered his room, Marcellus Aquilus was sitting on his bed waiting for him. Marcius's face was red from crying, and he was rubbing his bottom as he walked towards the general. In Marcellus Aquilus's opinion, Marcius looked absurdly young as he did so. Marcellus Aquilus's sons were younger than Marcius and he considered a beating now and again did them no harm.

And what else can a slave expect, he asked himself, especially an insolent one. If I owned him and he talked to me like that, I'd give him more than a caning; I'd give him a whipping that he'd never forget.

"Why don't you lie down Marcius," Marcellus Aquilus said.

Marcius lay carefully on his side and Marcellus Aquilus gently rubbed his back for him.

"How many cuts did you get?" Marcellus Aquilus asked.

"About ten," Marcius said miserably

"It sounded like your mistress made a thorough job of it," Marcellus Aquilus said.

Marcius sniffed.

"Now. Don't cry any more, Marcius. I'm sure you've had worse beatings than that," Marcellus Aquilus said.

Marcius remembered the prolonged beatings he had received from Atellus when he basically had done nothing to deserve them.

"But not from Auntie Flavia. She's never punished me before. And I didn't expect her to hit me so hard," Marcius said.

"She was making an example of you, Marcius. She wanted the other boys to know what to expect if they give her any cheek. It would not have given her any pleasure to punish you, Marcius. But you did ask for it. Never call a woman old or imply she wears too much make up. They don't take kindly to that sort of comment. And even if she cares for you, which I'm sure she does, you are her slave. You must not forget that."

The General was silent for a moment.

"Does it really disgust you? What you do," Marcellus Aquilus asked.

"Pardon?" Marcius asked.

"You said, 'You pay me to be disgusting.' Does it disgust you?" he asked.

"Sometimes," Marcius said. "When I'm tired and the client's old and takes forever."

"Old like me?" Marcellus Aquilus asked.

Marcellus Aquilus was tall, handsome, fit and in his forties. Some of the other youths were frankly envious that he chose Marcius so regularly when he visited the brothel. Marcius looked at the general in alarm.

"I didn't mean someone like you, sir. I just meant ..."

Marcellus Aquilus laughed.

"I know what you mean, boy. Don't worry. You gave me an honest answer to an honest question. It's not disgusting with your lovely Egyptian friend, is it?" Marcellus Aquilus asked.

"How do you know about that?" Marcius asked.

"Oh, Marcius, it's obvious from the way you two look at each other," the general said. "You like sharing his bed, don't you?"

"It's different. He loves me," Marcius said.

"Yes, I see. It's different with a beautiful young man who loves you. If you keep talking like that, I'll think you really are a girl," Marcellus Aquilus said with a smile.

Marcellus Aquilus gently touched Marcius's still sore bottom, Marcius looked at him anxiously.

"Don't worry," Marcellus Aquilus said. "I won't hurt your hot, little bum. Where's that ointment you boys use? If I put it on your stripes, it might be soothing, take some of the sting out."

"It's under the bed on my side. But would you do something like that for me?" Marcius asked.

"Why not? Do you think I never got a caning when I was a lad?" Aquilus asked.

Marcius rolled onto his stomach and Aquilus gently lifted up his tunic and pulled down Marcius's loin cloth. Then he gently applied to the ugly red marks across Marcius's bottom some ointment.

"Madam Flavia certainly gave it to you. Remind me never to annoy her," he said.

Marcius had to smile at the thought of Madam Flavia taking her switch to one of Rome's more important men.

"See, things are not so bad," Aquilus commented. "She has a temper like all red heads. She'll be back to normal tomorrow."

The ointment did help ease Marcius's soreness. After a while, Aquilus eased Marcius onto his side facing him. Then he leaned over and kissed him on the mouth for the first time.

"Poor boy," he said.

He reached out to take hold of Marcius's penis.

"I'll do something to take your mind off your bottom, as long as you do it for me. There's something to be said for the habits of adolescence," Aquilus said.

Later, Flavia asked Claudia if she had done the right thing.

"Of course, you did darling," Claudia said. "What does your instinct and experience tell you? You can't let him insult you in front of people, and Clodia can't let him do things the other lads are punished for. It's not fair, and the others will end up hating him. You do see that, don't you? No matter how much you love him."

"Love him?" Flavia asked. "Don't be silly. It wasn't the 'old whore' comment I minded so much; I know what I am. It was the 'over painted' bit that really annoyed me. I think I use cosmetics well."

"Of course you do, darling. What would that brat know? He'd never seen cosmetics until he got to Rome. The way you paint suits you very well," Claudia said soothingly.

And Claudia was correct, as Flavia knew enough about cosmetics to use them skillfully. On the other hand, no newcomer to Rome, if they saw Flavia on her way somewhere, would ever mistake her for a vestal virgin.

CHAPTER 13

A few days later, Ptolemy asked permission for him and Marcius to go browsing in the market. It was late morning, and no clients would be arriving for a few hours. Ptolemy did not usually buy much, but he liked to look at jewelry as his father had been jeweler. Rome's jewelers encouraged the two polite, pretty youths into their stores and encouraged the Egyptian's interest in their craft. The two youths browsing also encouraged other customers into the store. Customers, especially ladies of a certain age as the jewelers tactfully expressed it, noticed the youths in the store and came in to look at them and then stayed to look at the jewels.

One day as Marcius and Ptolemy were chatting to a jeweler, two patrician ladies entered the store. Marcius and Ptolemy knew what was expected of them, and made way for the ladies. One of the ladies, Julia, was looking for earrings, and her friend, Lavinia, was helping her choose. As her friend spoke to the jeweler, Lavinia glanced at the two lovely young slaves. The two youths chatted briefly about a bracelet they were looking at. As they left the store Ptolemy said quietly to Marcius, "Well. You could save up for it, or get General Marcellus to buy it for you."

Lavinia looked surprised and stared at the backs of the two slaves as they left the store.

"Are you ill, Lavinia?" Julia asked.

"No, just surprised," Lavinia said.

Once they had settled their business, Julia and Lavinia settled in a litter for the short journey to her home. Lavinia smiled at her friend and said, "Don't worry, Julia. I just had a shock. I've seen the prettiest slave in Rome as people call him.

They don't exaggerate. I don't think I've ever seen a more beautiful, graceful slave; male or female."

"Oh, you know about him," Julia said.

"Yes. I hear the gossip. I see to it that I do when it concerns my husband."

"Don't you mind?" Julia asked.

"That my husband visits a pretty clean professional instead of keeping some slut in the slums, or bothering my maids? No. I don't mind. He's a healthy man and I'm not well. He has his needs. He never embarrasses me. That's all I ask."

"Don't you mind that he's seeing a boy?" Julia asked.

"Not really. Years ago I caught Quintas in the stables with one of the lads who worked there. He was so embarrassed and apologetic. I was upset, of course, and sold the slave. I should not have really. It was hardly the slave's fault. It's not like he could say no to his master, and that lad was very good with the horses. One thing about these boys, they don't think they can take my place just because Quintas sleeps with them now and again. They know their place. Besides, that young man looks pleasant enough."

"That's what I hear," Julia said excitedly. "Oh, I suppose I shouldn't."

"Go on. You're dying to tell me," Lavinia said.

"I have heard ... well ... people say that he has a pleasant personality to go with his looks. They say that Madam Flavia is in love with him herself, but I don't think so. She's far too sensible for that."

"You've met her?" Lavinia asked.

"Oh, at a couple of parties," Julia said vaguely.

“What interesting parties you must go to, Julia,” Lavinia said primly before she laughed.

Two weeks later, Madam Flavia found herself dining very discreetly with Lavinia. She was taken aback at this turn of events. Through Julia, whom she knew slightly, she had received a message from Lavinia, whom she knew not at all. Lady Lavinia was of the highest nobility and spotless reputation.

“People like that do not dine with people like me,” a stunned Flavia said to Claudia.

“Maybe she wants to know what her husband is up to,” Claudia suggested.

“But I can’t tell her. If I start talking to the customers’ wives; I’ll be out of business by this time of day tomorrow.”

“I know. It’s difficult, isn’t it?” Claudia said.

“Difficult is hardly the word,” Flavia said.

“I think that you have to go. A invitation from someone like her is like an invitation from a consul.”

“I wouldn’t mind that,” Flavia said. “I’ve met consuls before.”

“Oh yes. I had forgotten that,” Claudia said.

Both women found that they liked each other. Although so different in background and personality, they were both intelligent, experienced women who knew the way Roman society really worked. Flavia considered Lavinia a real patrician beauty and clever with it.

She’s common beyond belief, Lavinia thought. But obviously generous and good hearted. And she must be smart to come so far from nothing.

Once Flavia worked out that the lady did not seem to mind about her husband's relationship with one of her boys, she relaxed, but she did wonder what Lavinia really wanted from her.

"I just want to know what this Marcius is like," Lavinia said, "I'm curious."

"That's all?" Flavia asked.

"Isn't it enough?" Lavinia asked.

"You're not jealous?" Flavia asked.

"Only insecure people are jealous," Lavinia said. "Do I strike you as insecure?"

"No you don't," Flavia had to admit.

And Lavinia had reason to feel secure.

What important man in Rome doesn't stray from the marital bed from time to time, Lavinia once asked herself. Rome is full of tempting slaves, freed slaves, and prostitutes, she thought. A man would have to be made of marble not to be at least tempted, and Quintus is not made of marble.

Marcellus Aquilus and Lavinia's marriage had been arranged when they were both quite young. But they were both realists. They did not except great passion in a marriage, but mutual respect and companionship. They had achieved this. And they had had their moments of passion. But Lavinia was now tired out with childbirth and miscarriages, and she and her husband had agreed to no longer share a bed. But Lavinia did not like it when her husband slept with her maids.

"They get cheeky to me," she told her husband.

Then there had been an embarrassing incident with a freed slave woman who had decided that Marcellus Aquilus should leave his wife and children and live with her.

"Did you say you wanted a divorce?" Lavinia asked her husband sharply at the time.

"I have told her over and over again that I have not the slightest intention of leaving you," Marcellus Aquilus said. "But she seems to live in a dream world."

Lads, Lavinia told herself, especially experienced ones, seem to have more sense.

As they talked, Flavia realized that for all her poise and elegance, that the lady Lavinia looked tired.

How many kids is it? Flavia asked herself. About five in twelve years, not counting miscarriages. No wonder she looks tired, and I bet she doesn't want any more kids for a few years at least.

Flavia suddenly understood Lavinia's tolerant attitude to Marcius.

A professional like Marcius is no threat to a lady like Lavinia, she decided.

"What would you like to know about Marcius?" Flavia asked gently.

"I saw him in a jeweler's one day. He seemed a pleasant young man. He looks very gentle," Lavinia said.

"He is," said Flavia. "Despite everything."

"Despite everything?" Lavinia asked.

"He's been treated badly in the past. Most people would be bitter in his situation, but he's not. I promise you that he is not bitchy, greedy or demanding. I'm sure that he would never do anything intentionally to embarrass you or your husband. He does not trust people too easily, but I'm not sure that's a bad thing," Flavia said.

"In your occupation?" Lavinia.

"Living in this city," Flavia said.

Lavinia knew what Flavia was talking about and had to smile.

General Marcellus Aquilus went off on campaign to put down a German revolt.

"It's always the Germans these days," his wife commented to a friend. "It used to be the Gauls."

Lavinia took the opportunity to invite Flavia to her home more often. Flavia considered that she visited Lavinia discreetly. Claudia forbade her to take her red litter and made her wear her simplest brown dress, no makeup or jewelry and a cloak concealing her bright red hair.

"I feel like I'm going to someone's funeral," Flavia grumbled but she knew Claudia was right. Flavia also used the back door when she went to Lavinia's home. Lavinia was somewhat apologetic about this as she suspected that Flavia was even richer than she was. Flavia laughed and said, "I don't mind back doors and kitchens; I'm that sort of person. Besides, anyone seeing me entering your house would think I'm one of your maids or a seamstress. I don't have a reputation to protect, but a lady like you does, Lavinia."

One evening Ptolemy and Marcius dined at her home with Flavia and her daughters. Flavia's daughters no longer flirted with Marcius. Seeing the tender way he and Ptolemy looked at each other, they knew they were wasting their time. But there was one evening a friend of his mistress was also dining who Marcius did not know. This beautiful lady, obviously a patrician, asked him quite a few questions about himself. Once Marcius and Ptolemy arrived back at Flavia's club, Ptolemy could not help laughing.

"What's so funny?" Marcius asked.

"Poor Marcius. You're still so naive. You don't know who that lady is, do you?"

"Who? Madam Flavia's friend?"

Ptolemy sighed and said, "That's Lady Lavinia."

"Lady Lavinia. Lady Lavinia! The general's wife?"

Ptolemy nodded.

"But shouldn't she hate me? Shouldn't she want to poison me or something?"

Ptolemy shrugged and said, "Rome isn't Gaul."

"You can say that again," said Marcius.

So General Marcellus Aquilus returned from the wars. He went straight to his wife's bedroom but she was not there. He heard his children's laughter in his courtyard garden and was pleased to be home. In his garden, he found his wife, children and their nurse as he expected, but there were two visitors he did not expect. Marcius was playing some sort of marbles' game with his older children, and his youngest son was asleep cuddled against Madam Flavia's ample breasts.

Marcellus Aquilus glanced at Marcius who smiled back as if to say don't look at me. I don't understand it either.

"You're home, darling," his wife announced. "Our friends Flavia and Marcius have come for a visit this afternoon."

Marcellus Aquilus kissed his wife and in her face he saw love and understanding. Marcellus Aquilus ate his dinner without really tasting it as he was still rather stunned. Fairly early in the evening, he went to his wife's bedroom. His wife was having her long dark hair brushed by her maid. She dismissed her maid.

"Why?" Marcellus Aquilus asked his wife succinctly.

"Because I like them," Lavinia said. "Flavia is so good hearted and funny. While I was ill, she visited me nearly every day, despite the fact she has so many businesses to run. She always cheered me up," she said.

"You were ill?" he asked anxiously.

"Just a cold," his wife said. "You know how easily I catch cold these days. And Marcius has to be one of the nicest young men I've ever met. There's a truly pleasant nature to go with that lovely face, which, you have to admit, is somewhat unusual."

"So … you don't exactly ... er ... object to Marcius," Marcellus Aquilus said.

"I could not have chosen a more suitable young friend for you myself," she said.

"But won't people talk?" he asked.

"My poor darling," his wife said. "Don't you think people are gossiping now? Let them talk. It's our business. No one else's."

Some of Rome's stuffier citizens made disapproving noises, but Lavinia's true friends, who knew the reality of her situation, smiled and said, "Isn't Lavinia clever?"

He nodded, smiled and kissed his wife. They talked of other matters, mainly about their children. Marcellus Aquilus was about to wish her goodnight when she took his hand and said, "You don't have to go to your own room tonight."

"Are you sure?" he asked anxiously.

"Yes," she said. "I have been feeling stronger lately, and I have missed you. But you will be very careful, won't you?"

"Yes, of course," he said.

Thus, Marcellus Aquilus was in a good mood the next time he went to see Marcius. He had missed the youth's beautiful young body, and gentle touch. Afterwards, as they lay in bed together, Marcius rested his head on the general's chest. Marcius said, "You're in a good mood. Have you won money or something?"

"Better than that. My wife approves of you," Marcellus Aquilus said.

"Are you sure?" Marcius asked. "It's strange, isn't it? If my father had messed about with any of mother's slaves, she would have had her flogged."

Aquilus was about to say that Romans are not barbarians, but he stopped to analyze what Marcius had said. Marcellus Aquilus knew that Gaul did not depend on slave labor as Rome did, although he knew there were some slaves in Gaul usually captured from other tribes. But the only Gauls he knew of who had owned slaves had been chieftains. Chieftains in Gaul, Marcellus Aquilus mused as he looked at Marcius. Marcius had blushed. He was praying to his gods that in the future his mouth would check with his brain before it produced words.

"Don't ask me, General. Please don't ask me," Marcius said quietly.

And Marcellus Aquilus understood. He had assumed that Marcius was no peasant. A Gaulish peasant did not stand, walk, speak and read Latin the way Marcius did. He had worked out that Marcius came from a noble family.

One of my mother's slaves, the youth had said.

Certainly he's from their nobility, he might even be a prince's son, Marcellus Aquilus thought.

He smiled at Marcius.

"Keep your secrets, little Gaul. Gaul is at peace now. It doesn't matter who you are, or, who you were," Marcellus Aquilus said.

Marcius hugged the general gratefully.

But, as Marcellus Aquilus was leaving the brothel, he asked himself if Flavia knew about Marcius.

She's from Gaul, he thought. She must have some idea.

Marcellus Aquilus went to Clodia's office where Flavia was counting silver coins. She looked up politely as General Marcius came into the room.

"Yes, General?" she asked.

"About Marcius ..." he began.

"What's he done now?" she asked wearily.

"He hasn't done anything wrong," Marcellus Aquilus said quickly. "It's about who he is."

Flavia said, desperately trying to sound casual, "He's nobody. Just another slave from Gaul."

"But who was he before he was enslaved?"

Flavia sighed.

"You know. How do you know?" she asked.

"He said something about his mother owning slaves. How many people in Gaul used to own slaves? It wasn't exactly one of your customs," Marcellus Aquilus commented.

"No. Not many Gauls owned slaves, but Queen Neala owned a few," Flavia said.

"Queen Neala? Of the Parisii?" Marcellus Aquilus asked with surprise.

Flavia nodded.

"How long have you known?" asked Marcellus Aquilus.

Flavia smiled. "From the first moment I saw him. He's very like his mother when she was young," she said.

"You knew her?" Marcellus asked.

"I knew her by sight. All the queen's tribe knew her at least by sight. It was the sort of thing she took pride in," Flavia said.

"And you decided to save her son," Marcellus Aquilus said.

"I've done the best I can for him," she said.

"Yes, you have," General Marcellus Aquilus said. "Would you have done it if he had not been a prince?"

"Done what?" she asked.

"Bought him. Saved him from the likes of Atellus?" he asked.

"I would have bought him if he was a peasant like me. It was the right thing to do," Flavia said.

"I did not realize that you Gauls were so loyal to each other," Marcellus Aquilus said.

"We're not," Flavia said. "That was our problem. We were too busy fighting each other to fight Rome as well. That's how you conquered us. Don't you remember?" she said.

"Yes," said General Marcellus Aquilus.

"General. What are you going to do about Marcius?" Flavia asked.

"Nothing. Gaul is at peace now. No one cares about survivors. We have Germans to worry about now," Marcellus Aquilus said.

CHAPTER 14

This convenient arrangement worked for two years, until, in fact, Marcellus Aquilus accepted a posting as governor to an Eastern province. He gave Marcius quite a large sum of money as a parting gift. Ptolemy bought his freedom from Flavia after five years of working in her club. He managed to have enough money left over to buy a share in a business with one of Rome's best jewelers who was nearing retirement, and just happened to be from Egypt originally like Ptolemy. Due to years of experience, he surmised that Ptolemy was a born designer, and trained him in those aspects of his craft which he had not learned when he was apprenticed to his father. As usual, Flavia had stayed in contact with one her favorite boys, she patronized his store, and as she had a passion for jewelry, she was one of his best customers and mentioned his store to all her friends. Ptolemy also knew that she would always loan him money if he needed it.

"But she has no taste," Ptolemy said to his business partner one day. "She just likes big stones set in big flashy gold settings."

His partner laughed tolerantly.

"That's her style," he said. "She's big and flashy herself. She's a freed slave woman who's made money. You suit her taste, and lots of women like her will flock here. Save your delicate designs for aristocratic ladies."

A few months after Ptolemy started his business, Marcius asked to see Flavia in Clodia's office. Ptolemy walked into her office. Ptolemy had some money saved from his business, and Marcius offered Flavia what money he had saved while working for her for the last few years. Ptolemy explained, in his most businesslike manner, that he wanted Marcius to come into partnership with him in his business. Flavia knew that Marcius knew about as much about making jewelry as she did, but she knew that Ptolemy wanted his beloved Marcius to live with him, and help him in his business in any way he could.

"Do you have a silver coin, little Gaul?" she asked.

"Of course," he said.

"Put it on the table and slide it to me," Flavia said.

Marcius did so.

"You are now a freedman, Marcius," she said.

"But I can pay you more than that for my freedom," Marcius protested.

"Of course you can," Flavia said. "But I want you to take your savings and use them in your business with Ptolemy. You need money to buy gems and metals to work with, don't you, Ptolemy?

"Yes Auntie Flavia," Ptolemy said quietly.

"You will come and visit me, won't you?" she asked.

"Yes, of course," Marcius said.

Marcius and Ptolemy started to leave. Flavia thought, My beautiful lads are leaving me; they're men now. I might never see them again. I have to tell him.

"Wait Orin," she said.

Marcius stopped stunned as no one had called him by his real name in years. Ptolemy had no idea what was going on, and he was not helped by the quick, quiet conversation in their original dialect that Flavia and Marcius then embarked on.

"How do you know my real name?" Marcius asked.

"I'm Parisii like you. Didn't it ever occur to you that I'm from your tribe?"

"I know you're from Gaul, but, there's so many tribes. And you didn't say anything," Marcius said.

"I thought it safer for you that way. Your mother was my queen. I knew who you were the first time I saw you."

"Is that why you helped me?" Marcius asked.

"Not really. I think I would have tried to help any slave in your situation. People tell me I'm too impulsive, but it doesn't seem to have done me any harm so far. I know you're a prince, Orin. But don't think about revenge. Look around you. These Roman pigs are devouring each other now. Their wealth is built on misery – on our misery. That can't last forever. And when their walls and their mansions crumble, we barbarians will be the ones to pick up the loot. We've sacked Rome before, and we'll do it again," Flavia said.

Flavia would not live to see the fall of Rome, but she did live to see the assassination of Julius Caesar. While a struggle for power began and the rest of Rome's population panicked, she decided to hold a party. Her friend, Claudia asked her: "What are you celebrating exactly?"

"It's a Gaulish thing. We have to celebrate the moon goddess this time of year or it's unlucky," Flavia explained.

Even by Roman standards, it was a riotous party. Claudia had never seen Flavia so drunk and cheerful. At one stage, she turned to Ptolemy, who was as confused as she was, and said, "Do you realize we're the only guests here not originally from Gaul?"

"I noticed," said Ptolemy. "Marcius said it's something to do with their religion."

"Their religion involves chanting 'Fuck Caesar and fuck all Romans' does it?" Claudia asked.

"Is that what they're saying?" Ptolemy asked.

"I think so. They're so drunk it's hard to tell. Two things you can say for Gauls; they know how to enjoy a party, and they're very good at holding a grudge."

The major conspirators against Julius Caesar were eventually forced to flee Rome, but Atellus was not one of them. He had known what was planned, but been absent on that particular day in the Senate. This did not save him. Octavius Caesar and Marcius Antonius hesitated briefly when including his name on their death list.

"Mind you," said Marcius Antonius. "There's no real proof he was involved."

"He's in their faction. And he's the slimy sort who would have been told, but kept his mouth shut, and waited to see who wins. Besides, it's not as if anyone likes him."

"True, but," Marcius Antonius began to say.

"I hear he's rich as King Midas. Want to split up his property?"

"I don't really fancy pretty boys," Marcius Antonius said.

"He owns much more than his collection of pretty boys. Besides, they will sell well in the slave market. There's his estates and art collection as well."

"Why not?" said Marcius Antonius.

Two of Caesar's experienced veterans were sent with a select group of thick headed younger soldiers. They arrived at Atellus's mansion at daybreak. It was so early in fact that only Calcus, the cook, and Darius were awake and dressed and in the kitchen. Calcus went to the front door when he heard a polite knock on the door. Unaware that assassins can actually knock on a door politely, he unbolted it and let them onto the house. It was one of the last things Calcus was ever to do. He shouted out a warning to Atellus but was immediately cut down and stabbed as he lay on the mosaic floor. Lucretius and Darius stared at each other in the kitchen. The soldiers found them. Darius wore a cord with a slave tag around his neck, so it was not exactly difficult for the soldiers to work out that Darius and Lucretius were slaves.

"Where's your master, cookie?" the group's leader demanded.

"In his bedroom. It's the third door on the left after you go up the stairs," Lucretius said without hesitating for a moment.

"I'll show you the way, sir," Darius offered.

As they went up the stairs, the group's second in command said to its leader, "Popular with his slaves, isn't he?"

Hearing the commotion downstairs, Atellus had jumped out of bed and wrapped a blanket around his waist. Atellus and Pavo had shared Cleon the previous night and all three men had been still asleep and naked when the soldiers entered the house.

"Run!" Pavo shouted at Atellus.

"It's too late," Atellus said.

By the time the soldiers entered the room Atellus was standing with a blanket around him, resigned to death and determined to act with some dignity. Pavo would have liked to do the same, but he could not remember where he had dropped his clothes the previous evening, and he practically threw himself under the bed in the hope of finding his loin cloth at least. Cleon was so terrified that he was crying, whimpering and trying to hide under the remaining bedclothes. On seeing the effeminate frightened Greek youth in the bed, and seeing his slave tag, the group's leader knew exactly what sort of slave Cleon was. Even if he did not mix in illustrious circles, even he had heard about the fabulously rich Atellus and his collection of Rome's most beautiful slave boys.

"Where's …" he began to say.

"I'm Julius Porcius Atellus. I'm the master in this house. I'm the man you're looking for," Atellus said with considerable self control.

The veteran then noticed Pavo's bare bottom and legs underneath the bed. He almost laughed.

"Tell your slaves not to panic, sir. We have no orders to harm them, as long as they don't get in the way."

Atellus then did the only decent thing he ever did in his entire life. He gave Pavo a kick to his behind, and said, "Get out from there, slave. And stay still. These men will think I don't know how to train a slave."

Pavo emerged from under the bed and looked at his friend stunned, then he realized that Atellus was trying to save his life.

"Sorry, master," Pavo said to Atellus.

"Slaves," Atellus said to the veteran. "They're always pathetic, but what can one expect?"

"Nothing personal, sir," the veteran said. "Just following my orders."

"Of course," said Atellus.

The two older men could have hacked Atellus to death with their swords, but they considered themselves professionals not brutes, so they knocked him to the ground and the leader swiftly and expertly cut Atellus's throat. Then they left. Pavo went over to his dying friend and cradled him in his arms. If Porcius had still been able to speak, he would have said, "Mind the Persian rug, Vibius. It cost me a fortune."

Then Atellus died, and his only friend closed his eyes, then placed him gently on the carpet.

Pavo went back to the bed and finally found his loin cloth, tunic and sandals. He dressed rather slowly. But before he put on his tunic, Cleon said, "Wait, master. There's blood on your chest."

Cleon came over to Pavo and wiped most of the blood off with the corner of the bed sheet.

"Master?" he asked timidly.

"Yes, Cleon?"

"What happens now?"

"I don't know, Cleon. There may be a lull in the civil war, but it won't last. No one knows who'll win. But you should be safe. Those soldiers could have killed everyone in this house and looted this place, but someone has ordered them not to."

"Will you be safe, master?" Cleon asked.

"I don't think I'm important enough to be on anyone's death list. And no one would think of looking for a patrician where I live," Pavo said.

"I see, master. Good luck," Cleon said.

Pavo looked at the beautiful Greek slave.

He really does care if I live or die, but I've never really done anything to help him.

Pavo was unaware that, in his presence, Atellus had been less harsh with Cleon and the others than when he was not there.

"Do you wish to come with me?" he asked.

"I can't run away, master," Cleon said.

"Run away from whom? From what? Your master is dead. There will be chaos. No one is going to look for one poor man like me and one escaped slave. Besides, if anyone ever asks, I'll tell them Atellus gave you to me last night as a gift," Pavo said.

"I don't know, master," Cleon said.

At Atellus's invitation, Pavo had slept with Cleon many times, and, when alone with him, Pavo had never been cruel to Cleon. And Marcius had said something about Pavo being "not so bad."

They went to the kitchen and sat at the kitchen table. Lucretius poured them both two large cups of wine.

"Go on, sir," He said. "You're both as white as sheets. It might help."

Cleon, Lucretius and Pavo silently drank their wine. Darius did not join them at the table as he was stirring a cauldron of porridge for the dormitory slaves.

"The lads still need to be fed," Lucretius had said once he realized that the soldiers had left, and it did not look like the household slaves were in immediate danger. Darius did not mind, as doing something practical and dull like making porridge helped him not to panic.

"What do you think will happen to us slaves, sir?" Lucretius asked Pavo politely.

Even in this situation Lucretius remembered that Pavo was a free citizen, a Roman and a noble.

"Someone ordered those soldiers not to kill slaves or steal property. I'm sure they pocketed anything small they could quickly pick up, but they did not destroy anything. People know what a collector Atellus is ... was. Someone has his eye on his property," Pavo commented.

"What should I do, sir?" Lucretius asked.

"Lock up the house and bolt every door. Block and barricade entrances and windows. The mob will soon hear that Atellus is dead and might decide to loot this place. Only open up to someone in authority."

"And the lads?" Lucretius asked.

“Are they safe in the dormitory?” Pavo asked.

“It’s as secure as the house, if not more so. The master was concerned about runaways,” Lucretius said.

“That might, for once, work to their advantage. I know you’re a decent man, Lucretius. Those slaves are young and defenseless and not used to making decisions. They’ll be frightened and confused by now. Will you look after them until your new owner arrives?” Pavo asked.

Lucretius shrugged and said, “Someone has to do it. And what will you do sir?”

“My family were important once, but because I’m poor and live in a slum, people assume I’m descended from a freed slave owned by one of my ancestors. I intend to encourage that illusion. Oh, and I’d like to take Cleon with me.”

“Is that all right with you, Cleon?” Lucretius asked.

“Yes, I’ll take my chances,” Cleon said.

Lucretius wondered, but he decided it was Cleon’s life and his choice. And he would have someone to protect him.

“It’s your decision, Cleon,” Lucretius said.

Cleon and Pavo left. Lurcetius and Darius took a large pot of porridge to the dormitory. The youths in the dormitory huddled together in fear. Lucretius told them that their master and Calcus were dead, but that he would be in charge and protect them until a new owner arrived. After the youths had eaten, Darius helped Lucretius select the strongest and oldest among them to return to the house and start bolting doors and barricading windows and entrances. Lucretius knew there was sufficient food in the storerooms so that no one would have to leave the house for days. Lucretius then ordered the youths to build a funeral pyre in the garden, so the bodies of Atellus and Calcus could be burned. Lucretius considered that he might get into trouble for this later, but he did not like the thought of leaving two bodies to decompose in his master's bedroom or the cellar. There was no grief for Atellus or Calcus during these hurried, make shift funeral rites, but Lucretius soundly cuffed the first youth who sneered so the rest fell silent.

Lucretius only had to wait three days. Marcius Antonius did not come himself, as he was too busy, but he did send his wife. Fulvia arrived with a document, her own steward and bodyguards. Fulvia haughtily handed her document to Lucretius. Although he could read, Lucretius could not understand the document, but he knew an upper class lady when he saw one, and he was in no position to argue. He bowed respectfully, called her mistress and showed her through her new property. Fulvia struggled to hide her excitement when she saw Atellus's collections of furnishings, art works and jewels. She was even impressed with the slaves in the dormitory. All the young male slaves she saw there were, at least, all healthy, alert and extremely handsome; three she considered really beautiful. She noticed, with some relief, that none of the slaves seemed younger than sixteen.

Well, she thought. Atellus wasn't as big a pervert as some people said.

She turned to Lucretius and asked, "And where is the dormitory for the female slaves?"

"What female slaves, mistress?" Lucretius asked.

"There has to be some," she said.

"Not since the death of my master's mother," Lucretius said.

"Who did the cooking, serving and cleaning?" she asked.

"The lads, mistress," he said.

"What about nursing the ill?" she asked.

"One or two of the lads were trained to nurse anyone ill," Lucretius explained.

"What about sewing? Your master must have needed clothes from himself, and tunics for his slaves," she said.

"The master bought that sort of thing from a workshop in the market," Lucretius said.

Desperately trying to think of some use for her own sex in this odd household, she said, "What about sewing repairs?" she asked.

"Little Xerxes does that sort of thing. He does lovely embroidery, too, although the other lads tease him about it."

In fact, Xerxes would have been teased unmercifully if not for two factors. Darius, who had established himself as boss in the dormitory regarded Xerxes as his special friend, and he protected him. Lucretius also liked the dainty Persian slave, and any of the others who wanted favors from the chef (like extra food) had to be polite to the sewing boy.

"Which one is Xerxes?" Fulvia asked curiously.

A tiny, slight youth stepped forward and smiled shyly at his new owner. Even Fulvia, whose taste in males meant she was attracted to males who were, frankly, more obviously male, stared at Xerxes.

She told herself what an exquisite child he must have been.

Xerxes had been an exquisite child born into the household of a bored Persian princess who lived in exile in Rome. He had been treated by her as her pet and being sold to Atellus later had been a rude shock to him. He was lucky that Atellus found him dull and stupid, so he did not have much to do with him. But Atellus kept him longer than he usually kept a slave because he considered Xerxes an artist with needle and thread.

Fulvia remarked to her husband later, "I've heard of a man preferring boys, but there was not one single woman in that household. That looks like fanaticism."

"Or hatred," replied her husband.

Fulvia sold almost all of Atellus's possessions at public auction as she considered she had enough slaves and her husband needed money as usual. But she made an exception in the case of Xerxes. Fulvia was as tough a matron as Rome ever produced, but like most people, she had to relax sometimes. Embroidery was her hobby and it relaxed and soothed her, and she was very skilled at it. She, like Atellus before her, soon discovered that Xerxes was brilliant at this craft. Xerxes was descended from generations of embroiderers who had belonged to Persian kings, so she really should not have been so surprised. Fulvia kept Xerxes for years, and only sold him due to financial problems, but she did make sure that she sold him to a friend who she knew would treat him well. Lucretius once said to Darius, "Don't worry about little Xerxes. He's the sort of person who if his entire village was hit by an earthquake he would be the sole survivor dug out of the rubble, and, even then, he'd only have some scratches on his arms."

"Yes," said Darius. "But his first questions would be 'How do I look?' and 'My face isn't marked, is it?'"

"Well," said Lucretius tolerantly. "It is such a cute little face."

When Cleon arrived at Pavo's room in a slum, he looked around. Cleon was a slave and had lived in some very basic conditions himself, but he had never really believed that someone as well groomed and well dressed as Pavo was as poor as he said. The room was also messy and dirty. Pavo saw Cleon's cool look and laughed.

"I did warn you, Cleon," he said.

Cleon knew to be tactful in this situation, so he said, "I can tidy and clean this room for you, master. I'm good at work like that. It will look better then, and be more comfortable."

"Yes, Cleon. You're right. I never seem to get around to tidying up, but I don't spend much time here. But you don't have to start right now; start when it suits you," Pavo said.

"Yes, master," said Cleon.

It did not take Pavo's landlady long to work out that she had a new tenant. But she said to her husband, "How does someone who can just afford the rent, afford to buy and keep a slave? He doesn't look like he cost a few coppers in the slave market."

Her husband shrugged. "Maybe he got him as a gift. He has rich friends, doesn't he? What about that rich Senator he knows? He's always giving him presents."

"Like clothes. How many people give each other expensive looking slaves?" his wife asked.

"Who can understand rich people? Maybe he owed him a favor," the man said.

"I suppose so," the landlady said doubtfully.

The landlady soon cornered Cleon on the stairs one morning and got a story out of him. Cleon said that his owner had been a rich senator who had died recently and given him to his best friend in his will. The landlady did not ask how Cleon's master had died; at that moment in Rome's history, she hardly needed to ask. And she said to her husband, "The pretty little slave thinks that his new master will sell him soon, as soon as things settle down."

"It's a pity that the senator did not leave him money instead of a slave," her husband commented. "We'd have more chance of getting the rent."

"Be patient," his wife said. "That slave will sell for a good price. He is so pretty, and he has such good manners. And he speaks Latin well so he's obviously had some education. Pretty young Greek lads who speak Latin and Greek always sell well at the slave market, don't they?"

"That's what I hear," the landlord said.

"Pavo should be well off in future," his wife commented.

"Perhaps," her husband said cynically. "But he doesn't seem to have much idea of managing any money he gets. When he gets money, he spends it immediately, then he lives on bread and water until the next gift or loan."

"Not everyone is as careful with money as you," his wife commented.

Within a few weeks of living with Pavo, Cleon learned not to anger him. Without money and friends, Pavo felt bored, restless and cooped up in his tiny room during the day. As a result he became irritable with Cleon and would snap at him. Mostly, Cleon did not snap back and accepted an insult or a rebuke, but one evening quite late, Cleon was tired, hungry and not really thinking so he insulted Pavo back. Luckily for Cleon, the insult was in Greek, so Pavo did not understand it exactly, but he knew back chat when he heard it.

(Historians suggest that the phrase "Fuck off, you big Roman bastard" occurs in at least fifteen ancient languages, most of them, now extinct.)

Pavo stepped forward, grabbed Cleon by the upper arm to hold him still, and administered a short, sharp lesson. Cleon squirmed and yelped as Pavo gave his rather small bottom three tremendous smacks with his large right hand. After the third smack, Cleon burst into tears and whimpered, "Please, master. Sorry, master."

. Pavo stopped hitting Cleon, and looked at his frightened face. He took the weeping youth into his arms and held him. Cleon could not recall ever being comforted after a punishment by any of his previous owners. Pavo let the frightened slave weep quietly against his chest until Cleon calmed down and composed himself. They sat on the bed, side by side, but Pavo kept his arm around Cleon's shoulders. Pavo remembered Marcius, and realized just how lonely and frightened young slaves like Cleon and Marcius must feel most of the time. Pavo thought, At least Marcius was free as a child. Cleon has not even had that; he has always been owned and punished by someone.

"Cleon," Pavo said gently.

"Yes, master?" Cleon asked miserably.

"It's all right now. You've had worse than that. I've seen you get much worse punishments."

"I know master. But you're not like Master Atellus or Master Calcus," Cleon said.

"Yes, but you belong to me now. You're still a slave, and I'm your master. I want to be fair to you. I want to treat you decently. But don't forget what you are, and what I am," Pavo said.

"No. I won't forget master. I understand," Cleon replied.

"You'll get more than my hand across your pretty behind if you're insolent to me again," Pavo warned Cleon.

Cleon nodded and said, "Yes master."

When tidying and cleaning his room, Cleon had noticed, with considerable relief, that Pavo did not appear to own a whip or rod or anything like that, but he imagined that Pavo would be able to find quickly enough a belt or a switch to punish him with if he felt like it.

"Come on, Cleon. It's late and it's getting cold. Let's go to bed," Pavo said.

Pavo was quickly in bed, but Cleon undressed rather slowly.

"I hope you're not going to sulk now," Pavo commented.

"What? Oh no, master. I was just thinking about what you said," Cleon replied.

"That's good," Pavo said.

Cleon climbed into bed, and after a brief hesitation, cuddled into Pavo.

"Master?" he asked.

"Yes Cleon?"

"Please be patient with me. I need some time to learn what you expect from me. I've never belonged to someone I wasn't terrified of," Cleon said.

"I know, Cleon. I don't want you to be terrified of me. But I want you to do as you're told."

"I can do that, master," Cleon said.

Pavo went to sleep almost immediately, but Cleon found it difficult to go to sleep right away. He wondered if he had done the right thing in coming to live with Pavo. He had acted impulsively and now decided that he did not really know Pavo very well. He was kinder than his previous owner, but that was not exactly much of an achievement. He knew that Lucretius would have done his best to protect him, but Lucretius was not exactly in a secure position himself.

Slaves have no rights, Cleon reminded himself.

Even if Pavo was poor, he was still a free Roman citizen, and he came from an upper class family. And birth still counted for something in this society.

But, Cleon thought, Pavo was raised to be a slave owner. He has been trained to fight and kill or to inherit and then run an estate with hundreds of slaves. It's not really his fault that things did not turn out that way. I have to learn to bite my tongue when he tells me off. He won't ever thrash me like Atellus used to.

Four weeks later, Pavo began to think about selling Cleon. The slave was useful and good company, and as he got to know his new master he became more skillful at judging his moods, and knew not to answer back or argue. Pavo also appreciated Cleon's skills and enthusiasm in bed. But, without Atellus's financial help, he found it difficult to support himself, let alone Cleon as well. Admittedly, Pavo received his allowance from his uncle, but most of that went on the rent. The food they ate became very dull. Pavo who had been used to dining at Atellus's mansion nearly every day became bored. To be fair to Pavo, he did share equally with his slave the basic food they could afford to buy at the market every day.

Finally, after what Cleon was convinced was their tenth bowl of cabbage soup in five days, Cleon turned to his master and said politely.

"I think you have to sell me, master, before we both starve. Master Atellus did pay a lot for me, and I must still be worth something."

"I don't want to sell you to someone like Julius," Pavo said. "Besides to sell you, I think I'd have to prove I legally own you, and that could be difficult. And I don't really want to remind anyone that Atellus was my friend at the moment."

"I see, master," said Cleon. "There is another alternative. I can go back to my old trade."

"Trade?"

"I'm a prostitute. I was born in a brothel. My mother was a prostitute, and her sisters, and some of her brothers as well."

"Her brothers?" Pavo asked.

"When they were young. I am from Greece," Cleon explained.

"A brothel keeper would want to buy you outright," Pavo said.

"But some boys work the taverns, like the tavern your friend owns," Cleon said.

Pavo's favorite tavern was owned by an old friend of his from the army called Lucillius. The wine at this tavern was cheap and drinkable, and the food edible because the owner had something of a side line. Upstairs from the tavern, there were many tiny rooms, hardly more than cubicles, where the patrons, in return for a copper coin to the owner, could hire for a short period and spend some time with one of the pretty boys, who also came to the tavern. Although he was not interested in pretty boys himself, he was a tolerant soul.

"It's not my business to tell anyone who they should have sex with," he commented to his wife one time.

"Besides," his wife said. "Most of the lads are pleasant and polite. And they don't pinch my bum every time I take an order to a table. I prefer them to drunken, noisy sailors and soldiers," she commented.

Lucillius's wife had been raised in a much tougher tavern near the docks at Ostia, so she knew all about sailors and soldiers when they got drunk and amorous. Lucillius laughed.

"But I turned out all right in the end, didn't I, love?" Lucillius asked.

"Of course you did, you big idiot," his wife replied.

But Lucillius considered that he was a tavern owner not a pimp. He accepted a coin for the hire of his upstairs rooms, but any further financial arrangement he considered a private matter between the patrons of his establishment. Some of the youths who came there were freed slaves who basically had no other real way of making a living. Many free born Roman youths came there, too, whose families were so poor that their mothers did not actually ask their sons how they earned money, as long as they brought some of it home and it meant more food on the kitchen table for the whole family. But most of the boys who came to the tavern were slaves who arrived with their owners.

Lucillius tavern was not expensive but neither was it cheap and dirty. Lucillius, his wife and a couple of slave women who worked in the kitchen and serving area saw to that. Pavo was uncomfortable the first time he took Cleon there, but he did know most of the patrons.

I'm certainly coming down in the world, he thought. But it was Cleon's suggestion and I'm here to protect him if anything happens.

He was worrying unnecessarily for Cleon was in his natural element. There were plenty of good looking youths at the tavern but an effeminate Greek slave as lovely as Cleon had never been seen in that tavern before. Drinkers and pimps frankly stared at him, and whispered to each other comments like "Where's that little beauty come from?"

Cleon, when not chattering to other youths like himself, sat close to Pavo. From his simple tunic and humble demeanor it was obvious that he was the property of the tall, strong Roman man he was with. But Cleon could also flirt, chat and gossip like the other pretty boys. Cleon had long, almost black hair which fell in soft natural curls to his shoulders. He also had large dark eyes with the sort of long eyelashes which women envied. He had a way of smiling at a potential client as if he was unaware of the effect his lovely eyes, features and hair had on men, but he knew how to use his looks to full effect.

He overdoes the flirting a bit, Pavo thought, but I suppose he knows what he's doing.

It did not take long for a patron to come over to their table. He was a large, red faced, somewhat overdressed man but he looked prosperous. He spoke Latin with a strong provincial accent, but he was perfectly understandable. He told Pavo that he was a merchant. Politely, Cleon let the two men dominate the conversation while they had a few drinks together. Then the man asked how much to take Cleon upstairs and the men agreed on a price. The man handed a copper coin to the tavern owner, and then put a friendly arm around Cleon's shoulders as they went upstairs and found a small, vacant room.

"I haven't seen you here before," the man said as he started to undress.

"No. My master comes here regularly, but this is the first time he's brought me here," Cleon said.

"He should have brought you before. You're the prettiest Greek boy I've ever seen. You'll make a fortune for your master," he commented.

"What would you like, sir?" Cleon asked politely.

"Nothing elaborate, lad. Just a suck to start with. Then I'd like you to lie on the bed and let me poke that pretty little bum of yours. You are used to it, I assume,"

"Oh yes, sir. I'm used to it," Cleon said.

So Cleon got on his knees and sucked expertly the way his previous owners had enjoyed. The client was impressed with Cleon's skillfulness and gentleness. He stroked his hair and said, "What a good lad you are."

When he was ready, Cleon lay on the bed and let the client use him. Neither he nor the client were unused to such things, and Cleon considered the sex later as "fine in a domestic sort of way." When he had finished, the client was pleased enough to give Cleon a kiss on the check, more money than he had originally promised, and ask his name. He had every intention of seeing such a pretty, skillful youth again.

But as he dressed the client noticed with some concern some marks across Cleon's buttocks.

"Your master a bit tough on you?" he asked.

"Not really. I get a belting now and again but what slave doesn't?" Cleon said mildly.

The marks on Cleon had been left by Porcius Atellus, but Cleon decided the client did not need to know that about his past.

"How long have you been a slave?" the client asked.

"Always," said Cleon.

They went downstairs and Cleon discretely gave Pavo two silver coins which Pavo just as discretely put in a leather pouch.

"Good lad," Pavo said. "Was it all right?"

"Fine," said Cleon.

At the bar, the customer had a drink. The tavern owner asked, "How's the new lad?"

"A real sweetheart, and very reasonable when you consider how pretty he is. You should give him a try yourself sometime," the customer suggested.

The tavern owner laughed and said, "Have you met the wife? She's the jealous type. She'd cut off my balls and make me eat them."

After this first client, Cleon had a drink and, with Pavo's permission, went to chat to some of the other youths.

"There's always a fair bit of waiting around in this job," Cleon explained to Pavo later.

But Cleon was very popular this evening due to his looks and the fact he was new at that tavern. A wealthy looking upper class gentleman took Cleon upstairs next. As he was an older man it took him a while to reach a climax, and he even apologized for this. Cleon grinned and said, "It takes most men longer when they're more mature. It doesn't worry me, sir," he said.

The wealthy man paid him generously. Later in the evening there was an army officer. At the end of the evening, a young fit looking gladiator chatted to Cleon, but he did not seem to have any money. Cleon would have liked to have gone upstairs with him anyway as he was young and handsome, but Pavo looked at him sternly and said, "No. And don't be such a slut."

Then they went back to Pavo's room.

As Cleon slept, Pavo hid his leather pouch in the chest where he kept his clothes.

Well, I won't get rich at this rate, Pavo thought, but we might earn enough for the rent, decent food and wine, and some warm clothes in winter. Look at all the good Julius's position and wealth brought him. Sometimes there's something to be said for a quiet life in obscurity.

But he was pleased at the amount of money Cleon had made in one night, but he did wonder how Cleon did not become sore and tired.

He asked him about it the next morning. Cleon shrugged and said, "Years of practice, lots of ointment, and not every client insists on using my bottom."

Then they went to the food market. They bought themselves the usual foods that they had been living on such as bread, vegetables, nuts and fruits. But they also had enough money to buy foods such as oil, seasonings, olives, cheese, dried fruits, honey and wine, which, if all still simple foods would at least provide them with more variety in their diet. Pavo also let Cleon spend a little money on sweets from a stall. Pavo preferred fruit at the end of a meal, but he knew how Cleon enjoyed sweets.

And he earned the money, Pavo told himself, so he deserves a treat of some kind. They went for their evening meal to a tavern which specialized in dishes made from freshly caught fish and seafood. Neither of them had eaten meat or fish in weeks and appreciated a large serving of a well flavored fish stew. They walked back to Pavo's room with full stomachs and secure in the knowledge that, having careful stored away their morning purchases, that they would have enough food for days. Pavo knew he could probably make more money if he sold Cleon privately to a lecherous old man or a brothel, but he decided that a smaller amount of money coming in regularly might be preferable in the long run. Pavo realized that it was not simple food he objected to, but the monotony of the same simple foods eaten every day, day after day.

"There's always cabbage soup if things get worse," he said to Cleon.

Cleon could not repress a shudder. Pavo did not make Cleon work in the tavern if he said he felt ill or sore or tired. He also trusted Cleon's instincts if he was wary of a customer who approached him. Cleon was always careful of men who were drunk, but some men who came up to him, he felt were strange or odd, and therefore dangerous, and Pavo would find a polite way of discouraging these men.

But Pavo disliked being solely dependent on Cleon's income. Cleon did not see the problem as he considered Pavo his owner and protector, and he immediately handed over the coins he earned to him without thinking about it. But Pavo had dreams in which various of his illustrious ancestors would appear to him and say, "Vibius Menenius Pavo, you were not raised to be a pimp!"

"No, great ancestors," he replied in his dream. "I was raised to murder barbarians and steal everything not nailed down or wait for someone to die in the family and become rich that way. But it did not turn out that way, and I still have to live."

Lucillius helped Pavo without really meaning to. Lucillius had retired from the army after a leg injury. It healed, but he still had some pain sometimes, and his days of marching across Europe and Asia were over. Being a practical type of person he bought his tavern. But he did insist on doing work around his tavern that a man with an injured leg should not do, and inevitably, an accident happened. His wife, Junia, after saying a few times, "I told you so," put him to bed and made him stay there. Junia was good at running the tavern, but she was not literate and she only had two slave women to help her. She felt that a tall, strong ex soldier like her husband or Pavo were needed behind the bar to deal with any customer who became drunk and difficult. So she went to see Pavo and asked him to help as a friend until her thick headed husband is back on his feet. Pavo was not paid a wage, but took a share of the profits depending on how busy they were. Even after Lucillius was back on his feet, Pavo continued to help out in the tavern. He would have been there most nights with Cleon anyway, he reasoned.

As Junia said to her husband, "It's only fair he gets a reasonable share of the profits. He works behind the bar, he helps you get rid of trouble makers, and since he brought his little Greek into the place, we've been a lot busier. Most new customers come in because they've heard talk about a lovely new lad at our tavern, which means more lads come in, too. Cleon cannot go upstairs with every customer who wants to go upstairs with him. And there's plenty of other pretty boys they can choose if Cleon's busy. And they're all customers, which means they all drink and eat something."

Pavo did not think his ancestors would think much of his promotion from pimp to barman, but he felt better about it. At least both he and Cleon could now contribute to the small horde of bronze and silver coins in his clothes chest. Pavo and Cleon fell into a routine. They slept in, had a late leisurely, generous breakfast, then went to the public baths together. This was not just a matter of cleanliness and relaxation, but was also a means of free advertising. Admittedly, the tall, handsome Roman ex soldier and his slightly built, effeminate Greek slave made a handsome couple. Many men looked at them, a couple almost drooled. Decius Horatius Bassus whispered to a friend, "Slaves?"

"The Greek looks it, but the tall one walks like a soldier," the friend replied.

I know that lad from somewhere, Bassus thought.

Menenius Pavo worked out with weights while Cleon did the exercises fundamental for dancers which he had learned as a child. These exercises were such a part of his life that he did them every day except when he was ill. He found the routine of these exercises relaxing, and they kept his body in superb condition. After swimming and bathing, Pavo and Cleon sat beside a pool and relaxed. Pavo got into conversation with other patrons of the baths who while chatting politely could not help gazing at Cleon.

Bassus ordered the slave accompanying him at the baths to discretely follow Cleon and Pavo when they left. The slave returned to his master's home and reported to Bassus that he had spoken to the landlady and that Pavo and Cleon lived in a real slum. He said, "The eldest one is called Menenius Pavo. He's free but very poor. The Greek only came to live with him recently. They both work in a tavern nearby."

"Do you know which tavern?" Bassus asked.

"The name of the owner is Lucillius, and he's a friend of the tall one."

"I think I've heard of that tavern. It's a pity they're not both slaves. I might buy the pair of them. What name did you say again?"

"Menenius Pavo."

"Menenius Pavo? It can't be. You must have heard it wrong."

"Master?" the slave asked.

"That family is important, or it was. I can't imagine someone from that family working in a tavern."

"He could be a freed slave once owned by that family," the slave suggested.

"That makes more sense. He could be a freed slave or the son of a freed slave woman," Bassus said.

Most Romans slept with their slave women and fathered some of their children. And Bassus knew some men who, if particularly fond of a slave mother and child, would free them and have the child educated.

"Old Menenius Pavo was randy enough in his day. That man could not do anything in moderation. He had lots of kids with his wives as well as his maid servants. Interesting. What tavern did you say again?"

"Lucillius's tavern," the slave said.

One afternoon, after a good deal of persuasion, and some pouting, Pavo allowed Cleon to go to the market and buy some cheap perfume and cosmetics. Pavo did not really see the need for this in Cleon's case, but he later admitted that once Cleon had applied various lotions to his face and hair he did look even more beautiful than usual. He also noted how Cleon enjoyed pampering himself like this.

"You are vain," he said with a smile.

"Think of it as a business expense," Cleon said.

One evening, Pavo and Cleon arrived earlier than usual at the tavern to help Lucillius and Junia clean down tables, benches and the floor. By the time Bassus and his steward arrived, Pavo and Lucillius were behind the bar serving, and Cleon was sitting at a table chatting to a fair haired youth. The fair youth was showing Cleon a cheap, but pretty, bracelet given him by a customer.

A fair youth, Bassus thought. He reminds me of someone. You old fool. That dark lad is Cleon. One of Porcius Atellus's slaves.

Bassus and his steward went over to buy the two youths some drinks. He was in no hurry, and the lads talked pleasantly and politely to him. Cleon thought that Bassus looked familiar, but he was not sure where he knew him from. The fair youth was not as lovely as Cleon, but he was good looking and likable, so after speaking to their owners, he took them both upstairs. Bassus spent a pleasant time with the youths kissing, touching, watching them touch each other, before asking the youths to take turns sucking him. He paid both of the youths very generously.

Bassus came to the tavern twice a week after that. He saw Cleon regularly but other youths as well. He was always generous, pleasant and not very sexually demanding. He brought the youths small gifts such as sweets and trinkets. Some of the youths started to refer to him as "Uncle Decius." But, after a while, he tired of the noise and lack of privacy at the tavern.

I have got to the age when I prefer sex in the comfort of my own bed, Bassus thought.

So he spoke to Pavo about Cleon coming to his house for a visit. When Pavo hesitated he smiled and said very quietly.

"He'll be safer with me than he was with Julius."

"Julius?" Pavo asked.

Bassus continued smiling.

"Poor Julius," he said. "At least his little Greek found a protector. Whatever happened to that nice fair lad from Gaul? Do you know? What was his name?"

"Marcius. I do know. He was sold to Madam Flavia before Julius's death. Cleon told me."

"Good. Flavia looks after her slaves. She knows how to treat and get the best from a slave like Marcius. I'll tell you what. Come with Cleon to dinner at my home. I don't hold large parties these days, but I keep a good table for family and friends."

"Family?" Pavo asked.

"I have nephews and nieces and they have children. They visit their old uncle regularly. Mind you, my nephews work for me and are my heirs, so they like to humor me," Bassus said.

In fact, these nephews visited their old uncle from affection as well as duty. He had adopted them, educated them, and trained them in his business as an importer. Bassus intended to leave his considerable property evenly distributed to his nephews and nieces and hoped that they would not quarrel over money when he was dead.

"Decius Horatius Bassus," Cleon mused later. "Oh yes, I thought I knew him. He used to bring me sweets. I thought that was kind of him. He was a friend of Master Atellus, so I did not expect anything from him. What does he want?"

"You, I expect," Pavo said.

"He can have me any time he comes to the tavern," Cleon said.

"He might have in mind something more long term," Pavo said.

"Are you going to sell me?" Cleon asked anxiously.

Pavo saw that Cleon was genuinely upset at the thought.

"You know he would not be cruel to you. He's more likely to spoil you rotten," Pavo said.

"I know, but he's an old man. He can't live forever. What if his family dislikes me? They could sell me to anyone," Cleon said.

"Yes, they could. Don't worry. I'm not going to sell you. We can get by on what you earn and what I earn. We'll manage."

Bassus's home was not a mansion. He could have lived in a mansion if he wanted to, but he preferred a smaller, comfortable house run by a small staff of well trained slaves. Bassus appreciated fine food, and the meal he presented to Pavo and Cleon was almost perfect. Pavo ate heartily, but remembered his manners, and did not fall on the food with the sort of enthusiasm Cleon did.

"Cleon," Pavo said. "Don't gobble your food like that. You'll make yourself ill."

"Oh, sorry, master," Cleon said. "But this is my favorite dessert."

Bassus laughed.

"Let the lad enjoy himself," he said. "A healthy young man should have a good appetite. My chef made that dessert especially for him. He remembers how fond he is of it."

"Your chef, sir?" Cleon asked.

"Lucretius," Bassus explained. "You may go and say hello to him if you wish."

"Yes, sir. Thank you, sir," Cleon said.

Cleon stood up and quickly left the room.

"He's a little childish sometimes," Pavo said apologetically.

"But that's part of his charm," Bassus said. "And considering his past it's a wonder he's not totally bitter, selfish and cynical. I'm sure his charm has got him of trouble on more than one previous occasion. He could not have amused or charmed Atellus, of course, but I imagine he managed to distract Calcus when he was angry with him. And a few other previous owners as well. Do you often get angry with him?"

"Sometimes, but it's difficult to stay angry with him. He can be impulsive, but he does not mean any harm. He needs a slap now and then."

"I'm surprised you need to punish him. After belonging to Atellus, I should think he would be too terrified of any master to be disobedient."

"I don't want him to be terrified of me," said Pavo. "I want him to obey me because he understands some basic rules, and wants to please me."

"You want him to respect you and obey you; not just fear you. It's easy enough to frighten someone like Cleon into obedience, but respect has to be earned."

"How?" Pavo asked.

"Be fair to him and try to understand him. He has to feel safe with you, learn to trust you. Perhaps it's not too late for Cleon. He tried to help that other poor unfortunate lad, which shows he has some good left in him. He hasn't been totally crushed."

"He has many good qualities," Pavo said.

"Of course, or you would not have saved him when you thought he might be in danger," said Bassus.

"I saved him because he seemed to care what happened to me, although even now, I don't understand why he should have been concerned. I did not do much to help him when Julius owned him."

"You might have done something that Cleon appreciated, even if it might not mean that much to you," Bassus suggested.

"I tried to get Julius to calm down sometimes, when I thought he was going too far with one of his slaves. There was only so much I could do, I could try to influence him; but I could not tell him what to do."

"Cleon might understand that," Bassus said. "You could try asking him."

This conversation reminded Pavo of puzzling discussions he used to have when he was young with one of his tutors who came from Greece.

"You're confusing me, Bassus," Pavo said. "Are you sure you're not a Greek?"

Bassus laughed.

Bassus then asked if Pavo would sell Cleon to him.

"I'm sorry. I can't," said Pavo. "I promised him that I would not sell him."

"He dislikes me?" Bassus asked.

"No, it's not that at all. He appreciates how kind you have always been to him. He knows and I know that you would treat him well. But he worries about his future. He's only twenty, but he can't be a pretty dancing boy forever. Where will he be in ten years time?" Menenius Pavo asked.

"Where will any of us be?" Bassus asked. "It's a pity. I was going to offer you three thousand denarii for him."

"How much?" Pavo asked. "No. I'm sorry. But I gave him my word."

"I thought you might say that, so I have another suggestion. I know you're poor, Pavo, and it's not your fault. But because of your family, you cannot exactly go digging ditches for a living," Bassus said.

"Oh, I don't know. What's the pay like?" Pavo asked.

"It would not keep Cleon in sweets. You know that I am an importer, mainly grain from Egypt, but other foodstuffs as well. I own warehouses. Politicians come and go, but the people of Rome have to be fed. I'm a businessman. Rome will always need people like me. I can offer you a position working with my nephews."

"I don't know a thing about importing food into Rome," Pavo said.

"Can you read, write and do sums?" Bassus asked.

"Of course. I did have tutors when I was a boy," Pavo said.

"How fluent is your Greek?" Bassus asked.

"It's good now. It was a bit rusty, but Cleon tends to speak a mixture of Latin and Greek, so my Greek has improved in recent times. Although I have learned some expressions that I'm sure my tutors were forbidden to teach me."

"Think about it, Vibius. I am offering to train you in what I consider an honorable occupation. It could be a new start for you, an opportunity to become independent."

"Won't your nephews resent me?" Pavo asked.

"Why should they resent you? I have trained junior partners before. You're an educated patrician, the son of an old friend, and, frankly, you need an occupation. Why should they resent that? Besides there's a saying in my family, 'he who pays the bills has the final say.' If I tried to make a merchant out of Cleon they would probably resent that, once they stopped laughing, that is."

"And Cleon?" Pavo asked.

"I want you both to live here. I want Cleon for more than just bed. I want his company, too. As you say, he cannot be a pretty dancing boy forever, but he is also a very competent household slave. My steward is getting old like me. It's time he retired and trained a replacement."

"Cleon?"

"Yes, Cleon. You under estimate him. Being a steward would not be suitable for you, of course, but it's an excellent job for a freed slave."

"You'd free him?" Pavo asked.

"Yes, in time. If he works hard, learns the job, and is honest."

"I think he will be," said Pavo.

Pavo spent the night in a guest room while, as agreed, Cleon spent the night with Horatius Bassus. Bassus decided it was a little too late to do more than kiss, caress and cuddle the lovely Greek youth before going to sleep, so he said, "Cleon, I'm not as young as I used to be and it's late. We'll have some fun in the morning if that's all right with you."

Then he fell asleep.

All right with me? Cleon wondered before falling asleep himself.

When Horatius Bassus woke in the morning, he found that Cleon had cuddled up against him. Admittedly, it had been an unusually chilly night for that time of year.

He might just had been cold during the night, Bassus thought. But I'm not so sure. This poor boy appreciates it when someone treats him with some kindness. Cleon stirred and Bassus, in an unhurried manner, started to caress and kiss the sleepy youth. By the time they were finished they were both satisfied. Cleon, as a dancer, had the advantage when having sex, of a flexibility and suppleness that meant he could find sexual positions comfortable for himself and Horatius Bassus. Bassus being older and overweight, and the first to admit that he was not as nimble as he once was, appreciated Cleon's experience and skills in this matter. As he held him afterwards, Bassus looked at Cleon.

"I hope you liked that Cleon. I hope that I'm not too old and decrepit for you," he said.

"You're not that old, sir," Cleon said.

Bassus laughed. "Now you're being polite. I must seem an ancient old wreck to someone as young as you," Bassus said.

"I don't mind being with men your age, sir," Cleon said. "They're always more ..."

"Generous?" Bassus asked.

"Well, I was going to say more considerate, kinder," Cleon said.

"And generous?" Bassus asked.

"And generous," Cleon admitted.

Bassus smiled and gently stroked Cleon's soft, dark curls away from his forehead.

"I actually believe you, Cleon. I know you'd rather be in bed with your young, fit, handsome master right now. But I've paid for you, so you know what's expected of you. But you do like it when a man has some consideration."

"Yes, sir," Cleon said. "You've always been kind to me when you did not have to be. I'm a slave. You can do almost anything you like to me, anything you want, but you've always been kind."

"And a kind older man is preferable to a unpredictable, cruel young bastard I assume," Bassus said. They both knew

Horatius Bassus was referring to Porcius Atellus although his name was not mentioned.

"Is Menenius Pavo ever cruel to you?" Horatius asked.

"No," said Cleon. "He's not cruel. Sometimes he slaps me if I answer back, but that's all he ever does. I should not answer back, but I can't help it sometimes. He really isn't cruel, but he's been raised to be a slave owner, and I was raised to be a slave. No one can get away from how they were raised."

"No, maybe they cannot," said Horatius Bassus. "But they can think about it, and examine their own behavior."

Cleon looked puzzled.

"Sir?" he asked.

"I have asked your master to sell you to me for three thousand denarii. You know that's quite a sum for a slave, don't you?"

"Yes master. I know that."

"He refused despite the fact that he is so poor. I have suggested another arrangement to him. If you both come to live in this house, you can both work for me. Your master needs a job, something to do each day. I can offer him a respectable position with my nephews in one of my warehouses. And your job will be to be my companion. I promise that I'll never whip you or order you whipped. I won't humiliate you or give you to my friends. I'll be kind to you. I know that I won't live forever, but I'm a healthy man for my age and size. I can offer you years of comfort and security. And my steward can train you, so you will have a future."

"I couldn't be a steward. I don't read very well," Cleon said.

"That you can read at all is a good start," Horatius said. "Your mind is as agile as your body, but no one has given you the chance to use and develop your intellect. My steward is patient and efficient. He can teach you what you need to know about running a household like this one."

"I don't know," Cleon said.

"All I want you to do is try, Cleon. If it really is beyond you, I won't insist on you learning to be a steward. I want you to think about it. I don't want you to come to live here if you don't wish to," Horatius Bassus said.

"But if my master sells me to you," Cleon began to say.

"I want you to come here willingly," Horatius Bassus said.

Once they returned to the small, dark, damp room where they lived, Pavo and Cleon considered the fact that Horatius Bassus was offering them both the chance of a brighter future.

"It will be like having two masters," Cleon commented.

"Aren't you used to that?" Pavo asked.

"Yes. But it can be difficult. What if you give me an order, and Bassus tells me something different. Who am I supposed to obey? Who will punish me if I make a mistake, if I don't know what to do?"

"I would not punish you for something like that. And neither would Bassus. I'm not going to sell you. I will still own you," Pavo said.

From the beginning, the arrangement worked well. Pavo spent most days in Horatius's Bassus's various warehouses learning how his businesses operated from Horatius Bassus's nephews. Bassus visited his warehouses once a week or so, but he trusted his nephews to run his business smoothly. He spent his days with Cleon whom he found to be an interesting and pleasant companion. They went to public entertainments and the baths, browsed in markets and walked around the city. Bassus felt that walking was good for his health, and Cleon liked to accompany him. When he had been owned by Atellus he had rarely been allowed out of the mansion, and then, only, in Calcus's company. Cleon was now allowed to come and go as he wished, although Bassus did like to know where he was going and when he expected to be back.

After the first week in Horatius's house, Cleon asked Bassus if he could visit his friend Marcius. Bassus looked up from a scroll he was reading in his library and said, "I don't think you should go anywhere near Madam Flavia's club, Cleon. She might have you grabbed by one of her big bodyguards and not give you back to me."

"I don't think he works there anymore. I heard that Madam Flavia freed him, and he's trying to start some sort of business with a friend."

"Where did you hear that?" Horatius Bassus asked.

"At the baths. Boys like me, we do tend to gossip a bit," Cleon said with a grin.

"Yes, I've noticed," Bassus said. "What sort of business?"

"Jewelry."

"He should not be hard to find. I think I'll come with you. If their product is any good, I might buy something pretty for my nieces."

Horatius was always generous to his family. He particularly enjoyed browsing in the market with Cleon in search of small gifts such as sweets, games and toys for the small children of his nephews and nieces.

"I always knew that I'd never be a father or a grandfather, Cleon," he said. "But being an uncle and great uncle is not a bad substitute."

A couple of hours every day, Bassus spent teaching Cleon to read and write Latin. He was pleasantly surprised to find that as a child Cleon had been taught to read at a simple level in his own language, and that Cleon could also write in Greek the alphabet and his own name. Horatius found in his library the simple texts that his nephews had used when they were first taught to read and write by their tutors. Once Cleon had grasped the basics, Horatius found for him simple, short, amusing stories to read; the sort of texts a tutor would use with a bright young child. Horatius wondered if Cleon would find these stories too childish, but Cleon liked stories drawn from the Greek myths about heroes and gods, and the first time he completely understood a story without help from Bassus, he knew he had achieved something and was proud of himself for days. Horatius Bassus was proud of Cleon, too, especially the way Cleon worked quietly and diligently at his lessons. Bassus told himself, I don't expect him to be able to write plays or poetry one day, all I want him to be able to do is understand letters, business documents and accounts. If he is able to read stories for pleasure as well, that will be a bonus.

After a while, Lucretius showed Cleon how to keep the kitchen accounts, and later, Horatius's steward explained the more complicated accounts for the whole household. Both men reported to their master that Cleon grasped very quickly practical matters like numbers, bills paid, money owed, and lists of suppliers.

"Don't you find accounts dull?" Horatius Bassus asked Cleon.

"Well," Cleon said. "Your chef and your steward have shown me how they do the accounts, and it all seems logical and straight forward. It does not seem to take them that much time to do the accounts. Lucretius seems to like ordering food and planning meals. He said it's all part of the job, and it's the only quiet time he gets during the day."

Bassus would not have persisted in teaching Cleon to read Latin or understand accounts if he had been unwilling or he had not seemed capable of understanding such things, but he considered that Cleon had a good brain as well as a pretty face.

"Why do you bother?" Menenius Pavo asked Bassus one evening.

"Slaves just aren't that bright. If he asked me questions all the time like he does you, I'd get angry with him."

"Cleon is not stupid," Bassus said mildly.

But he was thinking, Cleon is capable of learning many things, but I'm not so sure about you, Menenius Pavo.

Cleon also continued to do his daily exercises in Bassus's courtyard garden, and Horatius liked to watch him.

Why shouldn't he be proud of his looks, Bassus thought as he watched him. And his lovely body which he keeps in such good condition.

When Cleon had lived in Menenius's tiny room he had been obliged to do his dancer's exercises and movement at the baths. He was so beautiful and graceful, that many of the bath's patrons had stared at him, and whispered to each other.

"Who is that? Who owns him? And where does he live?"

Not surprisingly, many of these men found out where Cleon lived, and became his regular customers when he worked in Lucillius's tavern.

Most evenings, Bassus would dine just with Pavo and Cleon. Cleon would serve the meal and then pour wine for the Roman gentlemen before joining Bassus on his couch. When Bassus had guests such as old friends or his family to dine, Cleon would go about his duties quietly and competently and then retire to the kitchen until the end of the meal. Cleon understood that he could hardly join Bassus on his couch when his family and friends were there, especially in the case of his nieces and nephews. As he commented to Pavo one time, "How would Master Bassus's nieces explain that to their small children? They're used to being waited on by slaves even at their age."

But, near the end on the meal, Cleon was often called back to the dining room to entertain Bassus's great nephews and great nieces. They were all very young and enjoyed the way Cleon could do tumbles, cartwheels and back flips for their amusement. Often they would join Cleon on the floor for a childish romp, much to the amusement of their parents.

But one night there was an accident. Livia, who was Bassus's eldest eight-year-old great niece, managed to trip herself up while playing in the game on the floor. She managed to put her hands forward, so she saved herself from falling flat on her face, but she hurt the palms of her small hands and she was shaken. She looked around for someone to blame.

"Bad slave!" she hissed at Cleon. "He tripped me, Daddy! You should whip him, Daddy!" she yelled.

Cleon knew that he had been nowhere near enough to the child to have tripped her, so he hissed back, "Lying little bitch."

All talk in the room ceased, as Bassus's family stared at Cleon. In their opinion, even if he had not tripped the child deliberately, a slave had insulted a member of their family. The girl's father stood up and took one step towards Cleon, but Pavo got to Cleon first and sent him sprawling with a tremendous clout to the side of his head. He then bent down to grab Cleon's now sore ear and dragged him into a kneeling position in front of the little girl.

"Apologize to the young lady, slave," Pavo growled at Cleon.

Cleon knew how much trouble he was in from the way Pavo was twisting his ear, and the stony looks from the table.

"Please," he whimpered. "I'm sorry, miss. I did not mean to trip you. I did not mean to call you that. I'm sorry, miss. I'm very sorry."

Pavo lessened his pressure on Cleon's ear to some extent.

"That boy deserves more than a sore ear for his insolence," the girl's father said. "He does not know his place. He deserves a beating. If you're not prepared to do it, Menenius Pavo ..."

"I'm prepared to do it. He's my slave. If you'll excuse me, I'll take him upstairs now and punish him,"

Pavo said.

Pavo let go of Cleon's ear, but he took a tight hold of his upper arm and started to drag him from the room. The child ran to her mother to be comforted and taken on her lap. Bassus hoped everyone would calm down now, but his youngest niece, who was only four years old started to cry.

"What's the matter, Antonia?" he asked.

"Cleon's going to get a spanking. I don't want Cleon to get a spanking. I like Cleon. You're the one who needs a spanking," she said as she stared accusingly at her cousin. "You're always getting people into trouble. Cleon said the truth! I heard Mummy tell my Nurse you're a little bitch."

Two sisters glared at each other. Bassus intervened before a full scale family row broke out, so he said, "Now girls. Calm down. I'm sure the little one misunderstood a conversation she heard. Come here little girls," he said.

The two little girls ran to their Uncle Decius, and he put one arm around the shoulders of his eldest niece, then his other arm around the shoulder of his youngest niece. He said, "Yes, Livia, Cleon was a bad boy. That was a very nasty thing to call you. His master will punish him for it."

Antonia started to sob again.

"No, he won't spank him, Antonia. He'll shout at him and tell him not to be so naughty in the future."

Luckily, for the sake of peace, more dessert was brought in from the kitchen by a kitchen slave sent by Lucretius, which immediately distracted the children, although their mothers were still glaring at each other. Horatius Bassus had seen a lioness fight a tigress in the arena once, so he had actually seen that sort of look before. Although he was concerned about what was happening upstairs at the moment, he knew that his primary duty was as a host, especially when his own family were his guests. As quickly as he could, after the meal was finished, he escorted his guests to the door. Once they were gone, he all but ran to his staircase and started to climb the stairs.

He had cause for concern. Pavo was so furious with Cleon that he had pushed him over his bed, held him still with one hand, and delivered a series of hard smacks to his bottom. The spanking had gone on for a long time, and he only stopped when his own hand started to sting badly, but he was still angry.

"Stay still, slave. I'm not finished," he snarled at Cleon.

Pavo looked around for something to beat Cleon with. Then he looked down at his belt. The belt he had worn that evening was a thick leather one. He started to take it off. Cleon looked at it in horror. Pavo's belt was elaborately decorated with pieces of shaped metal at regular intervals.

Cleon scrambled off the bed and looked at Pavo as he raised the lethal looking strap.

"Master!" Cleon screamed. "Look at that belt! You'll cut me to pieces. You'll kill me. Please don't kill me! Whip me tomorrow! Please! Whip me tomorrow!"

Whip me tomorrow, Pavo thought. Who said that?

Pavo looked at the belt in his hands. He had been too angry to notice how dangerous it was, to think how much damage it could do.

"I am not a monster," Pavo muttered. "I am not a madman. I won't behave like Julius."

Disgusted with himself, Pavo threw the belt away from him across the room where it landed at Bassus's feet.

After a few minutes of silence apart from Cleon's broken sobbing, Menenius Pavo looked at Horatius Bassus and asked, "Have you been there long?"

"A few minutes," Bassus said.

"You would have stopped me, wouldn't you?" he asked.

"Yes. I would have grabbed you or got in your way until you calmed down. I'm glad you came to your senses without that."

They both looked at Cleon who was lying crumpled up on the floor and sobbing pathetically. Pavo made a movement towards Cleon, but Cleon cringed in fear.

Bassus put a fatherly restraining hand on Pavo's arm.

"Wait. He needs time to calm down, too. Why don't you get some fresh air, and a cup of water while I look after Cleon," Bassus said.

Pavo nodded and left the room. Bassus bent down and gently helped Cleon onto his feet and to lie on the bed. He sat on the side of the bed and held Cleon's hand while Cleon wept until he was calmer.

"Are you hurt, Cleon?" he asked.

"My bottom's sore," Cleon mumbled.

"I'm not surprised. But nothing worse than that?"

"No, Uncle Decius," Cleon said.

"Do you want me to tell him to leave?" Bassus asked.

"Leave?" Cleon said.

"Leave this house and my employment," Horatius explained.

"But I'd have to go, too," Cleon said.

"No you wouldn't, Cleon. It's not like he's really your master," Horatius said.

"What?" Cleon asked.

"You're story isn't very believable, Cleon. Not for someone who actually knew Porcius Atellus. Why should he give you to his friend before his death? He did not know he was going to die. And giving you to someone whom he knew would treat you better than he did would have been a kind thing to do; and you and I both know that Atellus was incapable of being kind to anyone. Besides ..."

"Besides?" Cleon asked.

"You actually belonged to Calcus at the time of Atellus's death according to Lucretius, and he never gave anything away in his life. He would not give away a valuable slave like you. You panicked and ran away with Pavo, didn't you?"

"Yes," said Cleon.

"Why?" Horatius asked.

"Because he was different from the rest of Master Atellus's friends. He had to act tough when Atellus and the rest of them were around, but he was different when I was alone with him. Marcius told me that he was different with him, too. He seemed sorry for slaves like me and Marcius. And I was scared when Master Atellus was killed; I just wanted to get away from that house. I thought that Menenius Pavo might treat me better and give me more freedom than Master Atellus or Master Calcus ever did. I was not allowed to leave the house without Calcus when I belonged to them."

"I see," said Horatius Bassus. "And some freedom is better than none at all. It's difficult to say who owns you now, Cleon. If Calcus had died a natural death, I suppose you would be the property of his heirs. Did he ever mention any family?"

"No," said Cleon.

"And any property of Atellus's was confiscated by Marcus Antonius, although the legality of that is debatable. I suppose, as Porcius Atellus did have some cousins, they should have inherited his wealth. Mind you, they've left Rome which is probably very sensible on their part."

"So who do I belong to really?" Cleon asked.

"I'm not sure, Cleon. Would you like to belong to me?"

"Yes, Uncle Decius," Cleon said. "What about Menenius Pavo?"

"Do you want him to stay?" Horatius asked.

"Yes. I just don't want him to hit me again. I know I deserved to be punished for snapping at the little girl. I should not have called her a bitch. That's an awful thing to call a child. I would have apologized straight away, but I did not get the chance."

"Yes. I think that you would have," Bassus said.

"And I did not trip her. I was nowhere near her. She must have tripped over one of the other children's feet," Cleon said.

"Or her own feet. She's not the most coordinated child in the family. But she'll probably grow out of that. Her mother was the same at that age."

"How would you have punished me?" Cleon asked.

"I would have slapped you and ordered you from the room. For the sake of appearances I would have promised my family that I'd whip you later, but I would not have done it. I promised you that when you came here. Don't you remember?"

"I didn't really think you meant it," Cleon said.

'Why not?" Bassus asked.

"Well, you are used to owning slaves, and you're used to being obeyed. And you're only human and everyone loses their temper sometimes. I assumed you would whip me if you were really angry about something."

"I gave you my word," Bassus said.

"Your word as a Roman patrician?" Cleon asked.

"No, Cleon. As I'm not a Roman or a patrician. I gave you my word as the son of two freed slaves from Illyria, which is what I am," Bassus said.

"You're what?" Cleon asked.

"You heard me, Cleon."

"But your name, Decius Horatius Bassus. The Horatii ... they're famous ... aren't they?"

"I had to call myself something, Cleon. No one can pronounce Illyrian names here in Rome," Horatius Bassus explained.

"You old fraud!" Cleon said.

Bassus grinned.

"I might have promised never to whip you, little Greek, but I did not say anything about smacking your rump when you deserve it".

"Sorry master. I was just surprised."

"I know you were. Besides I probably won't spank you if you misbehave; I'm more likely to stop your sweets for a week," Bassus said.

"A whole week?" Cleon asked. "I'd rather have a spanking."

"I know you would," Bassus said, and then he laughed.

Pavo sat in the garden and collected his thoughts. Bassus's garden was small but well kept and cool on warm evenings. Bassus enjoyed his garden and took pride in it. When the weather was fine, he liked to work beside his two gardeners. Bassus sat beside Pavo.

"How is he?" Pavo asked.

"Sleeping now. That's youth for you. I let him cry for a while, then we talked, and now he's asleep," Bassus said.

"Like a child," Pavo commented.

"Well, we both know he does have a childish side," Bassus said.

"I did not mean to terrify him like that. Atellus used to treat him like that. I thought that I was better man than him," Pavo said.

"You are a better man. You realized what you were doing and stopped yourself in time," Bassus said.

"What if I had not looked at the belt in time? I could have scarred him for life."

"That belt would have cut Cleon's skin. That would have shocked you and you would have stopped," Bassus said.

"Are you sure?"

"Yes," said Bassus. "I'm sure."

"He won't ever forgive me," Pavo said.

"Yes he will. Although you don't deserve it, that gentle soul loves you. You can be impulsive, but you're not a bad man. Cleon knows that," Bassus said.

"Do you want me to leave?" Pavo asked.

"No and neither does Cleon. But you must not treat him like your slave again. Perhaps Cleon should sleep in my bedroom for a few nights or by himself in one of the other bedrooms for a while."

For the next few nights, Cleon decided to sleep in Bassus's room while he thought about his options. He was civil to Pavo during the day, but when the three men dined together in the evening, their conversation was somewhat labored. After four days, Pavo went to his bedroom in the evening to find Cleon already in his bed. Before he started to undress he said, "Is it all right if I get into bed with you?"

"It's your bed, master," Cleon said.

"Don't call me master anymore, Cleon. I don't think anyone believes that little story now. Call me by my first name when we're alone together," Pavo said.

"Do I know your first name?" Cleon asked.

"Vibius," Pavo said.

"Vibius? No wonder you prefer people to call you Pavo," Cleon commented with a cheeky grin.

Menenius Pavo climbed into bed and for a long time he and Cleon gently kissed and touched each other before making love.

Two weeks later on their usual morning walk Horatius Bassus led Cleon in the general direction of where his tailor kept his workshop. Bassus appreciated well made clothes for himself, but he enjoyed more buying expensive tunics which emphasized Cleon's good looks.

I don't really need any more tunics, Cleon thought but he did not say that to Bassus as he knew Bassus enjoyed giving him gifts. But on approaching the street containing the tailor's store, Bassus turned down a different street; one containing jewelry stores in fact. Cleon was puzzled at the smug look on Bassus's face.

Cleon followed Bassus into a jewelry store located in the front of a simple looking house. Marcius looked up from organizing a display of bracelets on a counter in front of him and stared at Cleon. Cleon stared back. Then they rushed to each other and hugged. Silently, they held each other for a long time. When they had belonged to Porcius Atellus they had only touched each other when ordered to for the sexual gratification of their master or his friends. Now they were free to simply hug each other for as long as they wanted. Ptolemy came into the shop and smiled. After a while he said, "Is there something you're trying to tell me, Marcius? Should I start dividing our goods and chattels? Such as they are."

Marcius let go of Cleon and turned to Ptolemy.

"This is Cleon, Ptolemy," said Marcius.

"I think I know who he is, Marcius. You've told me about your Greek friend, Cleon," Ptolemy said. Bassus smiled in a fatherly manner at the reunion between Cleon and Marcius. Bassus had always considered Marcius an exceptionally good looking young man, but now he considered him stunningly beautiful. He had heard rumors that when working for Madam Flavia, Marcius had been described as the most lovely slave in Rome.

But most people would consider my Cleon a close second, Bassus thought loyally.

Then Bassus looked at Ptolemy more closely.

First, second, and third, he thought. If that Egyptian was one of Falvia's boys, too, it's no wonder she makes money.

Marcius suddenly realized that Bassus was in the store.

"I'm sorry sir," he said politely assuming that he was Cleon's owner or protector. "I did not mean to ignore you".

Then Marcius stared at Bassus.

"Do you remember me, Marcius?" Bassus asked.

"Yes sir. Of course sir," Marcius said.

Marcius did remember Bassus. Bassus had been the first of Atellus's friends who Porcius Atellus had loaned him to for a night. Marcius had been terrified that his master's friend would find fault with him and that he would be punished later. But Bassus had spoken to Marcius calmly and reassuringly before taking him to bed, and had been gentle with him. On later occasions when he dined with Atellus he had spent a night with Marcius or Cleon depending on his mood, and both the youths agreed that Horatius Bassus was a "nice old boy." Although once Marcius commented to Cleon, "What I can't understand is how Horatius Bassus can be a friend of our master. What do they have in common?"

"I think they're negotiating a business deal. Besides, I think that Horatius Bassus is the sort of person who knows anyone who matters in Rome and goes to everyone's dinner parties."

"Sir?" Marcius asked. "Do you own Cleon now?"

"In a manner of speaking. Don't worry, Marcius. I take good care of him, and he takes good care of me. That's about right, isn't it, Cleon?" Bassus replied. Then he asked, "Tell me one thing, Marcius. Did you get any of the sweets I brought you, or did Cleon talk you into giving them to him."

"Master!" said Cleon pretending to be outraged.

Marcius laughed.

"I think we shared them most of the time," Marcius said.

Bassus smiled and said, "What I don't understand, Cleon, is how you don't get fat."

Cleon grinned.

A few years later, Ptolemy and Marcius were making a respectable business in the jewelry trade. They hired free laborers when they need extra help in the workshop or store, and Ptolemy intended to train apprentices sometime in the future. By this time, Cleon was established as Bassus's steward managing his city dwelling. Bassus was content in his declining years; he enjoyed working in his garden, reading in his bedroom or library, taking short walks in the city with Cleon's help, and receiving frequent visits from relatives and friends. During his final illness he was nursed by Cleon and the rest of his devoted household slaves. Cleon was tactful enough to always consult with his master's family, who appreciated the care that Cleon took of Uncle Decius.

Decius Horatius Bassus died just after his sixtieth birthday with his family around him, but Cleon sitting on the bed holding his hand.

"It's time now, little Greek," he whispered to Cleon while he could still speak. "You have made me very happy. And dying peacefully in my bed of old age is something not many rich men achieve these days."

In his will, he freed almost all of his household slaves including Cleon and Lucretius, as well as leaving them money to start in new careers. Lucretius did not start a new career, actually, he simply found employment as a chef to rich families who knew his reputation as one of the best chefs in Rome. Cleon had more difficulty in finding employment. He was an experienced household steward by this time, but most Romans tended to buy a household steward rather than hire one, and rumors that Cleon had been a prostitute did not help him find employment.

Predictably, Madam Flavia came to the rescue. Over dinner at her home one night she said to Ptolemy and Marcius, "Why can't he come into business with you two? Bassus would have left him some money in his will. Can't you always do with another pair of hands when you're busy?"

"Cleon doesn't know anything about the jewelry business," Marcius said.

"Neither did you Marcius until I started to teach you," Ptolemy commented logically.

"You would not mind, Ptolemy?" Marcius asked.

"Why should I mind? I like Cleon," Ptolemy said.

So Cleon moved in with Ptolemy and Marcius. Due to his previous experience, Cleon took over most to the responsibility for organizing their small household, although he did help in the workshop and store when necessary. They lived rather simply and tended to share the household work like cleaning and cooking. Even if they had been able to afford to buy slaves to wait on them, the thought never occurred to them.

"When it comes to looking after the house and garden, it's quicker and cheaper if we do it ourselves," Cleon commented one time.

But their life was not all work. Cleon had always been a slave, and he enjoyed his freedom to come and go when he wished and do what he liked. For the first time in his life, Cleon was free to choose his sexual partners, and he enjoyed going to the baths and certain taverns where he flirted with soldiers, sailors, gladiators and young aristocrats and frequently brought a guest home for the night. Ptolemy and Marcius soon became used to one of Cleon's friends staying overnight, and staying for breakfast in the morning.

Their neighbors gossiped a good deal about the number of handsome young men who visited the jewelers' house, and speculated endlessly about the relationship between the three young men who lived there. In fact, Marcius and Ptolemy shared a bed most nights, but it was not exactly unusual for either Ptolemy or Marcius to sleep with Cleon in his room some nights. Nor was it unusual for the three of them to fall into Marcius's and Ptolemy's bed for an enjoyable three way romp. Marcius considered that he loved both in slightly different ways. His love for Ptolemy was passionate and intense, but he considered Cleon his best friend who had saved him from loneliness and despair during that time when they had both belonged to Porcius Attelus. The fact that Ptolemy and Cleon actually became fond of each other helped avoid jealousy and tension.

One of Cleon's more regular visitors was Menenius Pavo. Pavo still worked with Bassus's nephews and if he would never be a brilliant businessman, he was honest, competent and very good at negotiating deals as he tended to speak to everyone as an equal no matter what their origins. Menenius Pavo had also married a wealthy widow a few years older than himself who was impressed with his good looks, considerable charm and impressive lineage. Theoretically, Menenius could have lived off his wife's fortune, but he had taken some time to achieve his independence, which he was not going to give up lightly.

I'm never going back to being a lapdog, he told himself.

Somewhat to his surprise, Menenius Pavo soon proved himself a fond father to his stepchildren and his own children who soon arrived in his life. But he was not the sort of man who could be entirely faithful to his wife, and his wife would not have expected such a thing. But as he did not have affairs with her friends, seduce their household slaves, or appear to be keeping a mistress hidden away in a flat somewhere, she did not complain if her husband was a little late for dinner some evenings. At this stage, Menenius Pavo considered he had a pleasant life. He worked managing a warehouse for Bassus's nephews in the mornings, had a snack in a tavern, spent a hour or so in Cleon's bed some afternoons before going to the baths or to his home for dinner with his family

There was a good deal of gossip about the comings and goings of the three jewelers as their neighbors referred to them. Three neighbors watched Madam Flavia's distinctive litter depart one evening and said, "Who is that lady?"

"You are new to Rome, aren't you?" her neighbor said. "That's Madam Flavia. She owns most of the taverns and brothels in this suburb, and a few other suburbs as well."

"What has she to do with the jewelers?"

"Oh, don't you know? Those young men a few years ago were Rome's most expensive Greek boys. And she owned them for a while. They made her a lot richer, and later they bought their freedom. Madam Flavia is a good soul; she takes an interest in her former slaves. She visits them regularly to see how their business is doing."

The third woman said, "My husband calls those jewelers the Queen of the Gauls, the Queen of Greece, and the Queen of Egypt."

"Queen of Egypt? Like Queen Cleopatra?" the more naïve woman asked.

"Oh, Queen Cleopatra knows nothing about sex compared to those lads," her more worldly neighbor commented.

THE END

About the Author

Anton Perrick lives in Melbourne, Australia, and has worked in education, publishing, marketing and the Australian film industry.

This is Anton's first work of fiction for STARbooks Press.